WITCHIEST CIRCUS ON EARTH

MAGICAL MIDWAY PARANORMAL COZY SERIES, BOOK #1

LEANNE LEEDS

BADCHEN PUBLISHING

Witchiest Circus on Earth
Published by Badchen Publishing
4500 Williams Dr., Suite 212-269
Georgetown, TX 78633 USA

Copyright © 2018 by Leanne Leeds

WITCHIEST CIRCUS ON EARTH

CHAPTER 1

SHADOWS MOVED OUTSIDE THE YURT IN THE FIRST-morning sunshine. Circuses, even paranormal ones, rose with the sunlight to ensure that everything was ready for the townspeople. Since my yurt was next to Hildegaard's Kitchen, the tent in the backyard that held breakfast and coffee for the tired paranormal carnies, this all but guaranteed my early rise.

Hey, *everyone* needed their coffee in the morning. Even paranormals.

The performers and workers groaned and chuffed as they made their way to the coffee tent. I grabbed a pillow and buried my head underneath to catch more sleep, but it was futile. Between the drums and laughter, a hundred paranormals groaning outside your yurt while you tried to sleep wasn't soothing white noise.

"Charlotte, you awake?" My best friend at Magical Midway, Fiona Brus, was always awake long before I rolled out of bed. Grunting, I stretched out from under the warm, downy bedroll into the brisk morning air as her soft Scottish lilt continued to poke at me through the canvas. "Come on, sleepy, it's a Saturday! The normals will show up soon, and I have to get to my pen. Flag's up! Let's move."

"I know, I know, just give me a second!" Yawning, I made my way out of bed and over to the mirror by my writing desk. Peering at my image, I shuddered at the state of my hair. And my skin. And my puffy eyes.

Ugh.

Each summer I turned up at Magical Midway looking presentable. My clothes were clean and pressed, my skin soft and bright, my eyes clear with no bags. By the end of the week, I had the permanently disheveled look of a carnival worker suffering from malnourished sleep deprivation.

Gnarled hair sprinkled with hay matted in random places on my head, while puffy eyes screamed a glaring need for a comprehensive supply of makeup I wouldn't have bothered to put on if I had it, anyway. "You may as well come in, it will take me a minute to make my hair presentable."

"No one pays attention to your hair, ya ken?" Fiona slid into the pavilion with a graceful glide. "No one cares about anything before coffee, and it'll be lukewarm by the time ye finish unsnarling that nest of wheat on your head."

"Says the woman who stomped on my foot when I left a wee, tiny, itty bitty knot in her tail."

"That was *different*," she argued as she plopped down on my bed. "Kelpies do not have snarls in their tails. That's just not done. You should know better than that."

I stuck my tongue out at Fiona and returned to working on my fine, golden hair so I could get to Hildegaard's before all my favorite coffee flavors for the day disappeared. It was a final day all around for both the Magical Midway and me. Tomorrow, the fair was tearing out to travel to its next town, and I was returning to my human life in Mickwac, Texas until the following summer.

Well, tearing out, or down, was a misnomer. I'd never been around for a move from one town to the next, but Uncle Phil said it was about as complicated as snapping his fingers. The Magical Midway was a paranormal carnival and circus, home to over a hundred paranormals and run by my Uncle Phil.

I always looked forward to getting back to my human life, though our family's connection to the Magical Midway was important. I couldn't deny that I enjoyed my single summer week here each year. Every year when I left the circus, it felt like I had barely arrived and settled in before I had to turn around and walk away from it all.

"Okay, I give up. Let's get coffee." Throwing my hairbrush down next to my bed, I wondered if Uncle Phil could magic my hair for me the way he magicked everything else. I hoped none of the cute centaurs would be at breakfast.

Fiona and I made our way out of the yurt toward Hildegaard's as the numerous inhabitants of the circus scurried this way and that way with waves, yawns, and good mornings. Despite being in their human forms, many moved with the grace of the creatures they represented when the throngs of humans showed up to visit.

"Charlotte!" my uncle boomed as he rushed across the expanse of the backyard. "Are you positive you don't wish to remain just a few more weeks? Or months? Or years?" His rotund body jiggled as he hopped up and encircled me in a bear hug. "I despise it when you take off, young

Charlotte. It's like we lose the shining princess that gives the Midway its luster, dear girl."

"I hardly sparkle when I'm here, Uncle Phil."

"Oh, but you do, dear girl, you do! I'm constantly telling Samson how this place shines just a little brighter when you are here."

"I think you're looking at the sheen of my nose."

Uncle Phil passed his palm over my face with a grin, and I felt a shimmery energy tingle along my puffy skin. My hands moved automatically to my knotted hair and realized it was now entirely coiffed. The wet gloss that appeared on my lips felt soothing over the cracked dryness that had been there just moments before. Uncle Phil could make a fortune in New York City doing makeovers. "Thanks, Uncle Phil. But I still can't stay. Even for the hour a day you would save me on makeup and hair."

I don't know why I lied and said I worked on my makeup and hair for an hour each day. I didn't. I didn't even own makeup that hadn't expired sometime back when I was in high school.

"You don't want to upset your brother," Fiona pointed out. Uncle Phil rolled his eyes and waved his arms in a dramatic show of annoyance.

"My brother. Pah! How he produced a lovely witch like you, I'll never know. Assimilation. What a horrible word," Uncle Phil spat as if a bug had just flown in his mouth. "Why would anyone want to integrate when they could live at the Magical Midway and stand out under the Big Top lights? You would make a beautiful lion tamer, my girl!"

Uncle Phil criticized my father's refusal to participate in or uphold our paranormal heritage for the hundredth time. "At least he allowed you to accompany us all these vacations, Charlotte. Though I wish you would remain with us for more than just one week a year. That's no time to get to know anyone or anything, dear girl!"

"I have to get back to the shelter, Uncle Phil. And you know Dad goes ballistic when I talk about going on a circuit tour with you."

"Yes, yes," the big man snorted, hauling out a garish, multicolored hanky to blow his bulbous nose in. "I will always try to keep you here, dear girl. At least a dozen times per trip. I truly believe that it would do you good. You're only half a witch living in the human world!"

I was only one-tenth a witch in my regular life at best, but I decided not to mention that to my uncle.

"At least let her get her coffee first before you work on her again." Fiona grabbed my arm and pulled me away from my uncle. He bowed as we progressed on to the coffee tent, and I waved as he melted into the multitude of morning workers.

Fiona and I lined up for our magical morning elixir. Mocha Elegance for her (not that she needed it), and Peppermint Pride for me (which I needed about a gallon of). As we parked ourselves down at one of the many picnic tables set out beneath the shade of the tent, my uncle's black cat, Samson, jumped on the table and cast an intent stare in my direction. "Not you, too, cat. Shoo. Let me drink my coffee in peace." The cat hissed at me and hopped off the table.

"I have to admit there are times I don't get how you can live in the human realm," Fiona observed as she sipped her steaming mug of chocolate coffee infused with an extra shot of elegance. "Don't you ever miss all this? Or wonder what it would be like if you stayed and learned more about being a witch?"

"I do, I guess." I skimmed around at the men and women that made up this traveling family and swallowed the lump in my throat. I loved... well, most of those I knew. Some people were more challenging to embrace than others. The Larry brothers, who served as the security detail for the Magical Midway, were a little intimidating. Julius Larry stared at me from across the coffee tent as if he felt I had thought ill of him, and I quickly turned away.

Heck, maybe he knew my thoughts. How would I know?

My family had been so lax on my paranormal education as I grew up that I understood little of the paranormals that lived at this fair. With over one hundred paranormals, one week a year was not enough time to get to know everyone. It wasn't even enough time to familiarize myself with every type.

Turning back to find Julius Larry still staring at me, I nodded in his direction as his eyes narrowed in response. "This all seems so fantastical to me, though. Not like real life—and the paranormal world is so restricted, Fiona. What are you now, a few hidden villages and townships and some traveling fairs? It's such a limited world you all live in."

"First of all, it's we. Not me. We. You are one of us, too, Charlotte. It's not that bad, though. There are more than twenty towns in this country alone. It *is* bad for the carnivals and circuses, though. Only two traveling fairs left," she admitted. "The Langdons disbanded. It's just the Makepeace Circus and us now. I'm sure the Witches' Council is thrilled that we're all almost gone, but it's sad. I love this life."

"I know. In the human world, too, circuses are disbanding all over the place. It's a different time. Animals as entertainment are frowned upon pretty harshly, which is a good thing for the real animals. Puts you guys in a weird position, though." Fiona's expression grew sad, but she didn't argue with me.

There were so few paranormals left, and the human world had turned their…our practices and characteristics into Halloween costumes and comic strip figures. Why the mythological creatures and beings would want to gather as one tribe was easy for me to understand. I just wasn't raised that way. I didn't want to stay in the past with them and define myself as only a witch. My parents believed the human world, living as humans, is where our destinies lay.

On the days when I left, I did sometimes feel a pull, though. Like a whisper just beyond the range of my hearing. Once back home, I put the Magical Midway out of my mind, and the murmur eventually went silent. Perhaps if I stayed longer than a week, it would have grown louder, but I never did, and so it never did. *No doubt my father's plan all along*, I thought.

"Magic still has significance. Always will. You'd know if you stayed here long enough to get more than a hint of who we are. Who *you* are, Charlotte."

"You guys always do this to me on my last day," I said. I sipped more Peppermint Pride, hoping the elixir would bolster my resolve to leave without regrets again.

"You're going to be thirty next year, Charlotte," Fiona pointed out. Tilting her head, she stared at me. "Don't you think you're old enough to decide for yourself to stay longer than a week?"

"Of course I am! Dad's asked very little of me, though, and this is important to him. It's not about being allowed or not allowed, you know? It's about respecting him and what he believes. It's what he wishes."

"You're not a djinn, you don't have to grant anyone wishes. I don't get you. You can't date humans because of your talent, you haven't even moved out of your parents' house. I mean, Charlotte—what if your soul mate is on the

Midway? What if by not staying you're condemning yourself to be alone?"

A satyr walked by our table and discharged a tremendous fart. The coffee tent erupted in protests. Fiona and I exploded into a coughing fit as the walking stink bomb laughed and roared at the hilarity of the reaction to his thunderous bodily function.

"Never mind. Enjoy your trip back to Texas, Charlotte." Fiona choked as she flapped her hand in front of her face. "I can't make any persuasive argument after that. I give up."

I nodded while holding my nose.

Packing my things back at the yurt, I thought about what Fiona had said. Every time I had to leave this place I considered anew what it meant, why I was doing it, and what could change in my life if I stayed.

Growing up as a witch and the only daughter of two witches had been nothing…well, mysterious or witchy or anything. It barely registered as anything special on my radar.

My father was bound and determined to treat

our witch heritage as nothing more than expertise we had, like playing the piano or being math geniuses. He was insistent that being witches was not who we were, not the *foundation* of our identities. I was raised the same way secular friends of mine might be raised by ex-religious parents.

Sure, our family *was* Catholic. Yep, our family's *ancestors* are Jewish. We *descend* from witches.

Little incidents and facets of our lives were colored by that history, but there was no coordinated attempt by my parents to instruct, train, or develop my understanding of being a witch. We treated that facet of who we were with a shrug of the shoulders and concentrated more on the specific talent we each had because we were witches than the fact that we were paranormal. They also focused those extraordinary talents toward benefiting the ordinary mortal world.

Admittedly, we had some cool gifts.

Well, my parents did, anyway.

My father could telepathically speak to any living thing. He called it a spirit connection—if something had the spark of life, he could talk to it and it could speak to him.

Dad worked with his power enough to block

it out when he needed to, like when trimming the lawn. (The grass becomes seriously annoyed at any attempts to manage it or shape it into human neatness. It would *prefer* to be munched on by whatever random creatures are hungry and be left alone to grow wild. Thousands of blades of grass complaining in teeny, tiny whines of protest is deafening, Dad said.)

Mom could affect the emotions of anything around her. This came in handy as I was growing up. I suspect her talent is responsible for the steady, calm relationship I had with my parents all the way into adulthood. As teenage angst raised its snarky head, and I complained, freaked out, or got indignant, Mom would turn me down a notch or two. It allowed me to be reasonable at a point most teens were bouncing off the walls and drowning in waves of internal conflict.

As I grew up I recognized I could sense qualities, I guess. I couldn't get clear communication like Dad, but I could sense the truth of what someone was revealing. I could also sense emotions, like Mom, though I couldn't change or influence them the way she could. While my parents could read and control and speak to rooms of people or fields of grass, I was limited to a single being at a time and depended on proximity for it to be of any use.

I *knew* things, but I could not *change* things. I never went to the Witches' Academy to learn wand work, flying, or anything of that nature. Perhaps I would have the power to influence those around me if my parents had taught me just a few of the typical witch things like spells, incantations, and potions.

But they didn't.

So I couldn't.

Incidentally, this talent made dating *impossible.* It's why I still lived with my parents at twenty-nine years of age. Blonde, blue-eyed, not hideous looking—yet I found myself on the cusp of becoming an old maid because every relationship I tried to start ended within three dates.

That's right. Not an exaggeration.

Three dates were all it took for someone to lie about something important. Heck, at least fifty percent of prospective husbands got knocked out when, upon discovering I work at an animal shelter and rescue, they announced with enthusiasm they *loved* animals—and I knew instantly they were full of it.

In the human world, this lack of craft education, history, and training didn't bother me.

I lived like any other human—except for one thing. I was able to tell that every mean girl was a liar before she opened her mouth. I knew every charming, flirty boy was full of beans.

I had my parents, though, and the constant ebb and flow of animals that needed help for companionship. I didn't think often about my complete ineptitude as a witch. I never thought about the fact that my life was frozen in my teens, that precipice of womanhood I could never quite jump off of, even though I kept looking for it. At nearly thirty, I still lived at home, and I had never had a real relationship.

Ever.

For one week of the year with my uncle, though, I was in awe of the things I saw around me. For a small slice of time, I wondered what my life might have been if I had been raised to be a paranormal and not a human. I tried not to dwell on the fact that I went from a young adult life waiting to happen to the illusion of childhood.

Because that would have been depressing.

If it had been up to my parents, I would never have known of the Magical Midway. My uncle fought for me to get a small peek into my heritage as an Astley. He was determined that I have at least a small taste of paranormal life.

He almost beat up my Dad to get it for me, too.

Uncle Phil and my father were as different as night and day. While my father was critical and scornful of the paranormal towns and enclaves that kept the "real" world out and the "fairy tale fake" world in (his words, not mine), my uncle was a big, boisterous showman who basked in the paranormal world. He could wave his plump hand or twirl his mustache, and a yurt would accommodate more inhabitants. Uncle Phil could rearrange the Midway, create a new circus set out of thin air, or manifest my favorite meal from my favorite coffee shop in Texas with a wave of his hand.

On my thirteenth birthday, he showed up at my party with a gift and an agenda. The gift was a dazzling crystal circus elephant. The plan was to convince my parents I needed to create a bonding tie to the Magical Midway.

"You cannot cut her off, Alan," my uncle proclaimed as he shook his finger at my father. "She has to know where she came from! Give her to me for summers so she can learn about the Midway. There are few of us left with the blood tie after I go, and they are all *in this room.*"

"She doesn't need to understand the Midway, Phil. That's your thing, not ours."

"It's *our* thing, our family business, you right stubborn old goat! The Midway pays for your mortal mission in life, or did you forget?"

"Gentlemen, there is no need to raise your voices in the house," my mother soothed as a wave of calm washed over the living room. "Let's all discuss this calmly and rationally like adults. You're sitting right across from one another. No need to shout."

"Your husband is not rational, Martha," Uncle Phil pointed out coolly to my mother as her wave of *calm-the-heck-down* reached him. "I'll likely be around for years and years after all three of you are gone because of your stubborn determination to live this mortal life, but we should always be prepared for the unexpected."

"Phil, stop that. You'll scare the girl," my father stated serenely.

Around and around they went for hours, as calm as two Buddhist monks discussing nirvana, while I sat on the floor and nibbled at my birthday cake until they agreed. One week a year, and only that, I would visit Uncle Phil at the Magical Midway so I could get a taste of life at the paranormal circus.

I would do a job that didn't involve learning any new magic, and I would not be allowed outside of the protection of the fairgrounds.

I was packing up for the seventeenth time, having spent a little over four months of my life at the Magical Midway. Leaving was always just a dash awkward, making me feel as if I had scratched the surface of something I would never understand.

Which was, again, conceivably Dad's goal all along.

Samson wandered into my tent and hopped up on the bed. His eyes slow-blinked as he watched me, and I scratched him behind the ear. "Until next year, Samson, huh?" The sleek black cat whined in response, and I felt a wave of longing hit me. "I know. I'll miss you, too." The wave of longing shifted into one of contentment as I sighed.

Time to go.

"I'm back!" I called into the house as I dropped my bags by the door. My mother's Pomeranian, Puff, ran up to me on his teeny tiny legs and yipped while wagging his tiny tail. "Anyone here besides Puff?"

"On the back porch!" My mother's face pressed against the kitchen screen as if shoving it that extra inch inside would ensure that I heard her. I breathed in the heady scent of charred burgers, and my mouth watered as I made my way toward the back door.

"How was your week with Uncle Phil?" My mother wrapped her arms around me and pulled out a few strands of hay that traveled with me from Magical Midway. "I see you were working with the kelpies again."

"Yep. The week was grand, same as always. Uncle Phil added a seer and a mentalist to the lineup, and a Haunted House. They moved from the Langdons about midway through the summer, and Fiona told me Langdon Circus disbanded. I didn't get to meet them, though. Maybe next summer there will be even more folks, who knows."

"The Langdons disbanded?" My father stepped onto the deck from the backyard and leaned over to give me a quick peck before sitting down at the picnic table. "Did Fiona tell you why?"

"No, but I imagine it's the same issue with all

the circuses. Everyone's against circuses with animals now, so they probably ran out of money or something."

"But there are no actual animals at any of the magical circuses."

"Well, they can't very well explain that to the humans, Alan," my mother pointed out.

"No, I suppose not. I assume my brother is doing well?"

"You know, you *could* go visit him, Dad."

"But then he would get me to set foot in that damned carnival of his. I've been winning the bet for twenty years, and I'm not about to lose it now."

"Oh, Alan," my mother sighed as she walked back over to the barbecue to flip over the sizzling burgers. "You and Phil are so ridiculously stubborn."

I picked up a sweet gherkin pickle from a bowl on the picnic table and popped it into my mouth as my parents teased each other. Looking out over the back deck toward the animal shelter that my family ran, I listened. There were far fewer dogs barking than there had been when I left.

"Where is everyone? I don't hear the usual cacophony of barking coming from the cages."

"Your father came up with a brilliant idea early this week, and it's worked out magnificently. Alan, tell her!" My mother beamed at my father, and I suppressed a laugh as my father's expression turned positively sheepish.

"Now, Martha, it wasn't all my idea. Well, Charlie, we started a therapy dog training program for some dogs that couldn't find homes. The trained dogs were donated to a program that provides therapy dogs to underprivileged children that needed them. We shortened the wait list by forty-two!" My father smiled proudly.

"Wow. That's great, Dad. I can't believe you could get that done in such a short time. It sounds like half of the population is gone. How did you train so many dogs in a week? Doesn't therapy dog training take months of work with the dogs?"

"Well, we had major adoption days, too." My mother raised her eyebrow at my father's answer. "What, Martha?"

"Tell her how you got them trained so fast."

"Now, Martha, there's no need to—"

"Your father helped the dogs with a little magic." Mom smiled and smacked my father's hand like a naughty child as my father protested. "He worked hard to hide it from me, too."

"I did not!"

"Dad, there's nothing wrong with that. It helped the dogs, and it helped the kids, so what's the problem?"

"I did not use actual magic!"

My mother laughed as she flipped the burgers and rolled her eyes. "He had a long talk with each dog to discuss the opportunities they would have and explained what they would need to do. After which, they all became cooperative and eager. Each dog passed the certification test in a single day."

"That's still not actual magic. And it was their own choice!"

"Which they could only make because you had the Dr. Doolittle magic ability and were able to explain what they needed to do."

"Well, I didn't have time to teach them all English," Dad grumbled as he turned red and stood up.

"Dad, I think what you did was wonderful. The important thing is the outcome, right?"

My mother nodded. "That's what I keep telling him."

"Enough, you two. See, this is why I don't tell you things." My father kissed my mother on the cheek and swatted her behind before going back inside. The screen door slammed just enough for

Dad to make a statement he was slightly annoyed.

"It *was* funny," my mother said. She closed the barbecue top and sat down next to me. "One morning I went out, and twenty dogs were all lined up with military-like precision in front of their cage doors. Sitting, no barking, just patiently waiting. I *knew* your father had talked to them. Well, that or it was the apocalypse."

"Why is he so defensive? I mean, we're not lifestylers, but we're not anti-paranormal, either," I glanced in the house to make sure he couldn't overhear. "Dad's never been so defensive about his talent before."

"I think your father feels that the more he rejects his gifts, the less likely he'll be called upon to use them in service to the Midway."

"Uncle Phil would never step down or even want Dad there for anything more than a visit. He loves running the Magical Midway. I can't picture him ever doing anything else."

"Neither can I," my mother agreed. She glanced over her shoulder into the house and leaned closer. "Your uncle has no wife, and no children, however. When a ringmaster leaves or takes an extended vacation, a new one must be chosen from the Astley bloodline. I suspect your father is trying to make sure he does nothing that would encourage your uncle to take an extended vacation or change careers."

"It has to be an Astley? Who's qualified to be considered?"

"Just you and your father right now. Unless your uncle finds someone and has children, you and your Dad are the only ones that could step into that role."

"Well, what if we don't? We can both just say no, right?"

"Then the Magical Midway is dissolved. That's what likely happened to the Langdon Circus." My mother glanced at the sky as she contemplated the Langdons' demise. "The heir refused, or there was no heir and the magic that allowed the circus to operate dissipated when it wasn't passed on. That would be my guess as to what happened. The familiar can only hold on to it for a certain amount of time before it burns them up. When they go, it goes."

"Oh, wow. I had no idea." I contemplated what would happen to all the paranormals that lived at the Magical Midway. Plus what would happen to the Astley Animal Shelter? Over seventy-five percent of our operating budget came from Magical Midway profit. They were able to magically manifest so many things a carnival would generally need to buy that the circus raked in the money.

"The circuses, like the paranormal towns, are *old* magic, Charlotte. No one knows how they came to be, or why they have such power to protect the inhabitants. The paranormal towns endure because the power that protects them is rooted in the land, but the Midway's power anchors in a bloodline and a *person*. As people reject that life, there are no new nomadic paranormal fairs created to take their place. They disappear, the magic lost."

"That's really sad." I wasn't sure I could live always traveling, living in a yurt and always having all these weird paranormals around me all the time, but I loved Magical Midway. I loved that it was there for me, for all the people that loved living that life, and for all the humans that enjoyed visiting it. "Dad couldn't do that. As much as he doesn't like it, he couldn't say no if he had to do it."

"No." Mom shook her head. "No, he couldn't. And so he tries to reject magic, so Uncle Phil doesn't get any ideas about asking him to step in —and, no doubt, as a way to pressure him to settle down and contribute to the next generation of Astleys. The Midway protects the ringmaster, so Uncle Phil will be around a long, long time. I'm sure he'll settle down, marry, and have children long before this is a real issue. For now, it's just something for your Dad and Uncle Phil to argue about."

"Uncle Phil was alive and kicking when I saw him, so we should have nothing to worry about."

CHAPTER 2

MOM SURVEYED THE FRONT ENTRANCE OF THE shelter and smiled. Candles glowed ominously in the lobby of the building, and Halloween decorations covered every square inch of the place. "We outdid ourselves this year," she said excitedly. Mom skipped over toward the punch table and turned the paper skull just an inch to the right to maintain the perfection of symmetry that only she seemed to spot was slightly off.

"The place really does look awesome, Mom."

Each year, the Astley Animal Shelter put on *Animal House*, a cuddly alternative to the scary haunted houses that many younger children couldn't participate in.

Families in Mickwac and the adjoining towns would come here every year and wander through "scary" rooms like the Perilous Puppy Room and the Cavernous Kitten Cave. Donations raised went to the shelter, and many animals went home with their forever families after our Halloween extravaganza.

"Oh, my!" My mother fell against the wall and steadied herself as she erupted in peals of laughter. "The animals are so excited that I have to block them out a bit just to think."

"That's good. I hope Fang here is excited." I reached down and petted the three-year-old German shepherd with a limp. "I think he's going to find his forever home tonight." Fang wagged his tail and barked, shoving a wave of happiness in my direction.

So many animals had come in and out of our shelter over the years you would think I would've lost track of their memories as time passed. Each had such a distinct personality, though, that they made an indelible mark on my soul during their time with us. I could remember their names and their quirky little characters—and how happy they all were when they finally found families they loved that loved them back.

"Go check in the back and make sure that your father doesn't need help with anything," Mom directed as she continued pulling the tablecloth straight and moving plates one inch to the right or left to balance out the table.

Heading out toward the back of the central hall, I snatched a carrot stick from a vegetable plate as I passed. My mother sighed as she made an immediate beeline to the table to fix the tower of carrot sticks.

The sun was setting as I set out on the dirt path toward the kennels that would, at least for tonight, serve as a decorated cuddle playground for over a hundred costumed children. Compatible dogs had been gathered together in large rooms waiting for the evening to begin. Even though none of the dogs had been with us the year before and none could know what would go on, they yipped and yapped and barked in excitement.

"Hey, Dad, is there anything I can help you with?" Fang squeezed his large body through the entry with me to ensure that he would miss nothing. Dad was scurrying around moving the bags of dog food behind a curtained alcove to hide the day-to-day reality of an animal shelter away from the fantasy of the evening. "Can I grab any of those bags?"

"Nope, I've got it," he grunted as he slammed the last two bags on the pile. He pulled a purple curtain with black bats across the front and walked toward me to give me a hug. "Isn't this far better than some circus? Helping *real* animals instead of putting on a show that's all pretend?"

"The animals aren't exactly fake at the circus, Dad," I pointed out as we moved a bale of hay to create a pathway to the puppy room. "They just aren't fully animals, like, all the time."

Dad made a face and surveyed the kennels one more time, scanning to make sure nothing was out of place. If it was, he knew Mom would catch it, and he'd hear about it. Everything seemed marvelous, and all the dogs were brushed, fed, and happy.

"Oh, I know." Dad motioned for me to follow as he left the dog kennels and went toward the cattery. "I just can't imagine that you would leave all this."

"Wait, why would I leave all this?"

"No reason. I just had a weird dream last night. I've been having a few lately. Ignore me, kiddo. I get weird this time of year. Some witchy weirdness I can't shake, I guess."

As we walked toward the cattery, I glanced at my father, trying to understand the emotions I read from him. He was concerned about something, and there was a sense of foreboding emanating from him. Whatever the dreams had been about, they were enough to make my ordinarily steady father's energy feel stressed and confused.

Dad pushed the cat screen open, and we glanced around at the dozen or so cats and kittens that waited for the evening's visitors. They were cats, so their level of excitement about crowds of people that evening did not mirror the joy and excitement of the dog kennels, but the room seemed to hold a heightened level of entitled anticipation that even I picked up on. Dad had let them know the humans would be coming to visit with salmon treats for them all, and that piqued their interest.

A fat white tabby, Snowball, meowed at me inquiringly as she shoved an anticipatory wave of desire at me forcefully. "No, Snowball, not yet. I don't have any treats for you. They'll be here soon." The cat meowed disapprovingly and swished back to her favorite cushion in the corner while casting shade back in my direction.

"Ingrate," I told her.

"I think we're all ready," Dad announced as he took a last look around. "Let's go in and clean ourselves up. The volunteers should be here in half an hour."

I nodded and headed for the door, giving the cattery one last look around. I loved all the cats staying with us, but if this year resembled the previous one, nearly all of the cats in here would be leaving for their new homes within the next day or two. "Good luck, you guys!" I called as I walked out.

I didn't notice the soft shimmer of light in the cattery corner as I left.

~

"That was a fantastic night!" Dad danced around the lobby laughing, moments after the last guest left. The evening had been an exceptional success, with adoption applications for over forty dogs and cats. Mom and I had "interviewed" all the prospective adoptive parents and made sure they were good people with good intentions, checking with the animals chosen to make sure it was a match both ways. Even Fang had been selected by a family with a little boy who had a permanent limp just like the German shepherd, both obtained from a car accident that occurred when each was younger.

"It was wonderful, Alan. The dogs were wonderfully behaved, and we got a decent amount of donations this year," my mother concurred as she began cleaning up the lobby. "I'll take care of the lobby if you can get the dog kennels. I'm sure Charlotte can handle the cattery."

"I got it!" I called as I hustled out the door. The night was long, and reading so many people while doing the adoption applications had exhausted me. I couldn't wait to get done with the party wrap-up and get the heck into bed.

As I walked down the path to the cattery, a rainbow-colored sparkling light shimmered from inside of the annex, but…that couldn't be right. I didn't remember my father putting any Halloween lights inside the building. The cats weren't fond of weird lights or noises, and so the decorations within the place were minimal, and cat-approved. There was no way the cats would have supported the addition of the blinding disco-glimmer I was seeing.

I opened the door to find a cat in the center of

the room, sparkling. All the other feline inhabitants circled around the shimmering apparition as if they were getting a visit from grimalkin royalty.

"What the heck is going on in here?"

Indeed. It took you long enough to come out here and check on the cats. Especially after you allowed us to gorge ourselves to an obscene degree on salmon treats. What if someone choked? What if someone ate themselves into a stupor? the cat chastised as his audience turned their collective sullen stink-eyes toward me.

"Um. Did they?"

Did they what? the cat asked with some irritation as its glowing eyes narrowed.

"Choke or eat themselves into a stupor?"

Well, no, but that's hardly the point, now, is it? the cat asked as he tilted his head.

"Wait, how can I hear you talk? I don't have Dad's ability."

You do at this moment in time, the cat responded as it cleaned its whiskers.

"What point in time?"

This one. This point. This is a point in time. My goodness, you cannot possibly be one of the heirs being considered as a potential holder of the ring. I know witches are daft, but you seem to have daftness as your talent.

"Hey now! No need for insults, buddy." The cat was so sparkling and dazzling that I could barely see him through the shimmer. I could sense emotion coming from him, so I knew he was real, and he was there, but he shined so brightly that it was difficult to look at him. "Who *are* you?"

Samson.

"Wait, you're Uncle Phil's cat?"

Correction. I was your Uncle Phil's cat. Now, I am no one's cat. I am my own cat now that he is gone. For now and in this moment.

I scooped up Sparkles McAttitude and ran toward the administration building while clutching him tightly to my chest. To my surprise, the cat with the attitude didn't struggle against me, though I was hit with a wave of annoyance.

"Mom! Dad! We have a problem!" I burst into the lobby holding the disco-ball cat and nearly ran into my mother. Mom dropped the cup she was holding as she stared at the cat in my arms. Pale, her eyes filled up with tears. "He says he's not Uncle Phil's cat anymore, and that Uncle Phil is gone. What does this mean? Mom?"

My father burst through the back door and

stopped mid-stride as he glimpsed the glowing cat in my arms. "No," he whispered. My mother walked over to my father and gathered him in her arms, murmuring words of comfort as she held him.

You know why I am here, Alan, brother of Phil. Someone must bear the ring. I am here to find the next ringmaster. The only candidates are here.

"Dad, why can I hear Samson talk?" I dropped the cat to the floor and walked over to my father, who was now pale and white as a sheet. "I can hear his words as plain as if he spoke them. I can't *do* that."

"You can at the moment," my father choked out as he folded me in his arms. "Something's happened to your Uncle Phil, honey. I'm so sorry. So very sorry."

I felt my mother's warm hand rub my back the way she used to do when I was a small child, as my father squeezed me so tightly I thought my bones would bruise. "My brother has died. Samson has come so that one of us can be chosen as the next ringmaster. You and I are the only ones in the Astley family left, now."

Yes. So let's go. I'd prefer not to explode, thank you very much. Samson glowed brighter as he stared up at our family's grief.

"Jeesh, Samson, we *just* found out Uncle Phil passed away—what kind of a heartless jerk are you?" I hissed at the cat.

I'm a cat. What's more, I am the Astley family cat. We all have a duty, and my duty is not to incinerate myself. You must fulfill yours. We need to go.

"Samson's right," Dad sniffled and pulled away from me. His watery eyes stared into my eyes. "The Midway cannot go without an anchor for long. Samson can hold the Magical Midway's power, but not for much longer. You and I need to go with Samson so the ancestors can decide which one of us will become the new anchor for the Midway."

"Honey, you remember what I told you when you came home from vacation this summer? About the Midway needing a person to anchor through?" My mother grabbed my hand and took over for my distraught father. I nodded and squeezed her hand. "Well, Samson will take you and your father to the Midway so that your Uncle Phil can choose which one of you should take over."

We need to go. They are waiting. Samson hacked and then threw up a pink-tinged hairball on the floor. Dumbstruck, I stared at it and then glared at the cat.

"You were here during *Animal House*? And you didn't *say anything*?" I asked him accusingly.

I needed a snack. Traveling long distances while carrying cosmic power can make a cat hungry, Samson answered. I stared at him in shock.

"Honey, we have to go," Dad said quietly. I nodded.

"Good luck, you two," Mom whispered as Samson glowed even brighter and the rainbow sparkles whooshed around us. "I love you both, always, whatever you each choose and whoever is chosen."

The wind whirled around me as I wondered what happens next.

It was dark when my father and I manifested in front of Uncle Phil's yurt at the Magical Midway. The inhabitants of the circus whispered among themselves as we appeared. The Larry brothers stood guard at the four corners of the small clearing. Samson struggled to push away from me, and I gently placed him on the ground. He continued to glow with blinding brightness.

"Charlotte!" Fiona called as she raced toward me. Gallus Larry, the oldest of the Larry brothers, grabbed her startlingly fast by the arm and held her back.

"Stay," the Roman told her. "No one may approach the bearer candidates or the familiar until it is done. No one."

Fiona glared at him and shook her hand loose, stepping back to stand with the other kelpies, their faces lined with stress. The whole place seemed drained of the usual joy and excitement I knew from those that populated the circus. "Right, then. Get on with it, will ya?" Fiona snapped.

"The Midway is now in a time that is not a time, transported to a place that is not a place," Samson droned. The city lights that had glowed off in the distance when we arrived blinked once and then disappeared from view. A warm wind blew over those gathered. "Anyone who does not wish to witness the choosing may return to their tent."

"Can *everyone* hear the cat?" I whispered to my father. He nodded yes, without moving his eyes from the glowing feline, and swallowed. I grabbed his hand and squeezed, unsure of what was about to happen. My heart still ached for my uncle, and I was desperately confused. Everyone in attendance, including my father, seemed to wait with anticipation as if they knew what was coming next.

I had no freaking clue.

A shimmering bubble glowed, anchored at four points by four of the Larry brothers. It expanded until we were cut off from all those waiting and watching. Bob, the youngest, patrolled outside the glowing sphere while smiling optimistically at the attendees.

A pinpoint of light slowly glowed into focus within the center of the circle. As it expanded, it took the form of a rotund man. Features and details slowly focused themselves, and I realized that it was a glowing apparition of my uncle. I gasped as he smiled at me. Much fainter and slightly out of focus, a line of men stood behind him.

"Well, I seem to have relinquished the job earlier than I had hoped, my girl," Uncle Phil's shimmering image laughed as he acknowledged me. "Alan, nice of you to show up. Too bad it took my being murdered for you to actually visit the Midway."

"Murdered!" my father shouted. I saw all those outside of the bubble chatter among themselves frantically at my father's exclamation. Howls of anger and fury echoed within the bubble from every direction.

"Samson, turn the volume down on our soiree, will you? We won't get anything done with the peanut gallery rabble-rousing out there," Uncle Phil asked his cat. A deep silence descended within the bubble, and the protests of the audience were shut out in an instant. "There. Goodness, they can get themselves worked up into a tizzy, can't they?"

"Well, of course they're in a tizzy, Uncle. You just said you were murdered! Frankly, I'm surprised *you* don't seem that concerned," I told Uncle Phil as my father choked out a sob. Uncle Phil frowned at him.

"Actually, your father just said I was murdered, dear girl. Only you and your father and Samson can see or hear me. Now, Alan, don't get all emotional. We have things to decide and plans to make. I'll be concerned about my murder later. Right now, we have to get moving on this." My father smiled through his tears and nodded.

"Who is it going to be?"

"Well, clearly not *you*, Alan. You haven't been on this fairground in twenty years. Why would we choose you?"

"Charlotte has never even been formally

trained as a witch, Phil! You can't make her one of the two most powerful witches in the world with a snap of your fingers."

My uncle cast his eyes at me for a moment as I tried to absorb the news. Uncle Phil was dead, and he was about to hand the Magical Midway over to me. Tears filled my eyes as I took in both the death of Uncle Phil and that the circumstances of my life were about to change dramatically. It seemed like I should be panicking.

For some reason I didn't understand, I wasn't. Some part of me seemed to always know this would happen. I felt a strange sense of relief now that it was here.

I nodded, and my uncle nodded back and winked. Turning back to my father, I watched the two brothers engage in one last argument that didn't matter anymore.

"Well, I can, and frankly, who's fault is it that she will be woefully unprepared? It's not *mine*. *You* decided to pretend you were mortal and limit what she knew about the paranormal world. I warned you, repeatedly. How did you think this would work out when you decided *that*?"

"I thought you'd settle down like a grown up, get a wife, and have children so this wouldn't involve *my* family, you immature child!" My father's hands balled into fists, and his grief morphed into anger. He stepped up and stared Uncle Phil in the eye, furious at the fat ghost's amusement. The two men stared each other down, one angry and one bemused.

As moments passed and they continued to list each other's faults and poor decisions, my father's anger seemed to suddenly drain from him. He sighed. "I suppose none of that matters anymore."

"No, Alan, it doesn't. I didn't get myself murdered just to be able to tell you that I told you so. Though I have to admit it's an amusing afterlife reward. Because I *did* tell you so. Repeatedly."

"I'm more qualified than Charlotte. I was at least trained at the Academy. Choose me. Give me time to prepare her for the role."

"No. Our decision has been made," Uncle Phil told him without pause as the ancestors that stood behind him nodded. "You had your chance, and you knew this could happen."

"How on earth would I know this would happen? You have so many levels of protection around you that almost no one on the planet could possibly hurt you! Why would I think this was a *possibility?*"

"What do you mean, Dad?" My father shook his head and turned away from me, choked up again. I flicked my eyes to the shimmering visage of Uncle Phil. "Well? What does he mean?"

"He means that it really shouldn't have been possible for me to be murdered," Uncle Phil told me. "As the ringmaster, I'm darn near indestructible. My health should stand for at least a hundred years or more, and no violent act should be able to make a dent in me. I'm only sixty-five! Far too young for a ringmaster to die. The only person that can really hurt me is...well, me. And I didn't do it. I had a date with Jeannie Goldberg tomorrow to see that Broadway show everyone is talking about. I've been waiting two years to see that damn show."

"But then how are you dead?"

"I have no idea, dear girl," Uncle Phil said as his sparkling face grew more serious. "But I know that I am, and so we must get on with what we need to do. There's no help for all these regrets that your father has now."

As I stood in the glowing circle with my father, my uncle, and Samson, the reality that my uncle was dead slipped more profoundly within me. My father seemed defeated by the turn of events, while my uncle stood resigned but peaceful. I smiled at him again, and he smiled back. It was hard to mourn someone standing in front of you, even if that someone was glowing like a pink and blue disco ball.

"Dad, I'm okay with this. Really. You love the shelter, and you and Mom never wanted to live this paranormal nomadic life, anyway. I don't mind so much. I'm almost thirty, you know?" Walking over to my struggling father, I placed my arms around him. "Maybe it's *time* I moved out of the house."

"Charlie, are you sure?" Dad brushed the hair from my eyes as he called me by my girlish childhood nickname. "I feel like I have failed you. You know so little about the power you're about to get."

"She'll be able to contact me through Samson, Alan," Uncle Phil told my father reassuringly. "No ringmaster is ever *truly* alone. I'll take care of her, little brother. I promise."

"Oh, Phil," my father sighed. "I thought we would have so much more time, you and I." Dad walked toward Uncle Phil and stood in front of the older brother he never got along with but always loved. Dad nodded.

As I tried to ask what my uncle meant by never being alone (because that didn't sound so fabulous), Samson jumped on my thigh and wrapped his paws around me. The cat's long needle-like claws dug deeply into my flesh as lightning flashed in escalating rapidity from my uncle to the cat to me.

With a flash of blinding brightness, I heard a roar fill my ears as I collapsed on the ground.

CHAPTER 3

My head thrummed as the pulse in my skull beat a staccato inside my brain. Peeking out from beneath my eyelids, I glimpsed the candles flickering all around the tent I recognized as Uncle Phil's.

"'Bout time you woke up," Fiona snapped as she pulled the covers off me. "We've been stuck in the middle of nowhere for *two days now*. You have a bunch of right ticked paranormals waiting for your highness to drag your royal arse out of that bed and take us out of here."

Fiona handed me a Wake-Up coffee and grabbed my wrist to pull me into an upright position. "Not kidding, Charlotte, you have to get us somewhere that we can get supplies and sunshine. People are freaking out at being stuck in this pitch-black ringmaster no man's land. Not a good start to your reign."

Samson walked across the room and hopped up on the bed next to me. The black cat purred and rubbed his forehead against my thigh as Fiona waved frantically at me to drink my coffee faster. I sipped and squinted up at her while she glared at me. "What do you mean? Where *are* we?"

"Oh my herds, you must be kidding me. Don't you just *know?*"

"Um. I don't know. *Should* I just know?"

"I have no idea, but we're in this suspended no time no place thing. We have to get out. If you don't know how to get us back, you better ask the cat."

Think "next town." Samson's bored voice echoed in my head. *Phil always programmed the next three or four locations into the magic so it would be easy to move.*

As soon as I finished thinking *next town*, sunlight poured through the entrance to my uncle's yurt and an approving cheer went up through the grounds. Among the clapping and celebration, I heard several shouted epithets complaining about the time it had taken for "the blonde wench" to return the Midway to its proper time and place.

"Well, that was *rude*," I complained.

My father ran into the yurt and exhaled when he saw me sitting up and drinking my coffee. "Charlotte, I am so glad that you're awake." He crossed the living space and sat down on the bed next to me. "Is your uncle here?"

"Um. No. Uncle Phil is dead, Dad," I told my father slowly wondering if the time travel had rattled his brain.

"No, Charlotte, I mean is his *spirit* here. Or his ghost. I'm not exactly sure how this works, but I know that you should be able to call on him and talk to him. You need to start learning how some of this works, sweetie." My father appeared like he hadn't slept in several days. His shirt was wrinkled, and his face was stubbled. As I peered into his eyes, I noticed they were swollen red with deep bags underneath them.

"I don't really know, Dad, how this all works. But he's not here."

"Ask the cat," my father replied.

You know, I have a name. If we will be close family now, perhaps I would be more inclined to help you if you all stopped calling me the cat. My name is

Samson. My name is not the cat, the cat…er, Samson said telepathically.

"I apologize, Samson," my father said as he bowed toward the feline.

"The cat is already giving you lip, eh?" Fiona asked me.

"Can you not hear him?"

"I can only hear Samson because of my skill coupled with my bloodline, Charlie." Dad scratched Samson behind his ears, and the cat purred loudly. "No one else on the Magical Midway will be able to hear his words to you, though I suspect that he can communicate with the weretigers and werelions."

If I feel like it. I rarely feel like it, Samson responded as he swatted my father's hand away.

"So, Samson, can you call Uncle Phil here?"

Your uncle is already here. I can, if you wish, make it so you can communicate with him and that he can communicate with you.

"Okay."

My father, Fiona, and I sat silently in the yurt and waited. I glanced around for the pink and blue shimmering that had encased the outline of my uncle before he had passed his power on to me, but I didn't see it anywhere. The clock ticked the minutes away as the three of us held our breath waiting.

"Does it take a long time?" I asked Samson after three minutes.

No. It would only take seconds.

"*Would* only take?"

Yes. It would take seconds only after you asked.

"But I already asked."

No, you didn't, Samson disagreed as he curled up on the bed.

"Yes, I did," I insisted.

No, you did not.

I sighed in frustration as the cat closed its eyes and exhaled with contentment. Just what I needed, utter dependence on a small cat with a big attitude. "Samson, would you please allow me to speak with my uncle and allow my uncle to speak with me?"

My uncle's visage shimmered in the center of the room next to Fiona. As soon as he solidified he chastised the cat. "Samson, that wasn't very welcoming. I don't want you giving Charlotte a hard time. You are supposed to be helping her, not making her life harder."

You are not a ringmaster anymore, Samson thought as he opened one eye and stared at my uncle's flickering face. *What you want doesn't concern me.*

My uncle tsk-tsked the snarky little cat and turned. "Well, dear girl, I'm glad to see that you got the Magical Midway back to Earth without a problem."

"It wasn't that hard. Wait—Earth?" We weren't on the planet anymore?

"It wasn't that hard *this* time. The next two moves have already been set up for you, but the one after that will be a little bit more complicated."

"Are you talking to your uncle?" my father asked. I scanned back and forth between my uncle and my father. No one else in the room was looking at him.

"They can't see you?"

"No, my girl. Only you and Samson can communicate with me from the land of the living." My uncle smiled sadly as he gazed at his brother on the bed. My father seemed to comprehend that Uncle Phil was beyond his reach as the ghost spoke.

"I can't see him, can I?" my father whispered.

"No, Dad, I'm sorry. Only me and Samson."

My father's head dropped to his chest as tears rolled down his cheeks. "I thought I might get to see him again. Everything happened so fast during the ritual that I never told him that I loved him. And how much I would miss him. And how sorry I was that we didn't spend more time together."

"Tell your father that I loved him, too," Uncle Phil told me quietly. "We will see each other again. Just not for a while."

"He said he loved you, too, and you'll see each other again." My father hugged me and kissed my cheek, smoothing my hair from my face. Nodding, he leaned back and smiled sadly.

"At least you will get to spend time with him. Though I didn't want this, now that it's here I have to admit I envy you a bit. You are about to start on a wondrous adventure, Charlie. Do you want me to stay for a while?"

I shook my head no and stood up from the bed. "I think I need to do this on my own, Dad. You need to get back to Mom. She must be worried sick."

"I suspect she knows this takes a while," Dad smiled. "Any possibility I can get an express teleport back to the house, then?"

"Um. I don't know. Can I do that?" I studied Uncle Phil, and he nodded.

"Yes, child, you can. You must ask me

specifically to show you, and once you make the request, I can do so."

Taking a deep breath, I asked Uncle Phil to show me how to send my father home to my mother. Uncle Phil directed me to put my hands on my father's shoulders, close my eyes, and picture him back at home. Once I had that firmly in my mind, say the word *home*.

"If you need me, I'm here for you, Charlotte. I love you."

"I know, Dad. Love you, too." I hugged my father one last time, stepped back and placed my hands on his strong shoulders while picturing him at home with my mother and all the animals he loved. "Home," I whispered and my hands fell in the air as my father disappeared.

"I don't know what to do first," I told Fiona and Uncle Phil as I stood in the center of the pavilion. "I don't have any idea how to do this."

"That's why I'm here, my girl. Samson and I are here to make sure you don't make too many mistakes and to help you with what you need to learn."

Besides, I have your ringmaster training shield on.

You won't be able to kill anybody or relocate the Magical Midway to Egypt accidentally, Samson pointed out. *As your familiar, I can keep you from doing too much damage. Well, any damage actually damaging. If it's merely funny, I plan on letting you trip and fall on your face for my own amusement. Think of it as payment for the extra work you are about to put me through.*

"Gee, thanks, Samson," I told him with some exasperation. "Glad to know I can count on you to help me avoid murder but not humiliation."

"Samson is your familiar, but he is still a cat," Uncle Phil pointed out. "They're not the kindest, most empathetic animals the universe ever manifested into being."

"Can I trade him in for a dog familiar?"

"No." Uncle Phil and Samson both said at the same moment.

"It is very odd standing in here with you and listening to a one-sided conversation. You sound downright crazy, Charlotte," Fiona observed as she watched me carry on a conversation and question thin air.

"I think talking to myself might actually be more productive in this situation."

"Yeah, I always thought being half animal was probably easier than having to work with a full one. And it's a *cat*," Fiona mused. "The big werecats are pleasant enough, but I'm not sure I would want to go and have a beer with them."

"Don't big cats actually, like, eat horses?"

"Bite your tongue, Ringmaster."

"That still sounds so strange," I told Fiona as I walked toward the flap that would lead me out into the Magical Midway. "It's hard for me to believe that Uncle Phil is dead. Granted, that's partly because he's literally right here following us."

"Has he told you what on earth happened to him? I thought nothing could harm the ringmaster until he chose a successor and decided to move on."

"No, but what does that *mean*? How can someone not be able to be harmed?"

As we all stepped into the sunshine outside the yurt, Fiona slammed out with a fist and cold-cocked me. Her hand bounced off my face as if my features were encased in iron. There was even an odd metallic echo as if she hit solid metal armor. She then pushed me hard with both hands, and it felt as if anchors had grown from my feet and plunged into the earth beneath me. I stopped walking and stood, shocked.

"One night we should get some mead and test

all the ways that you can't be harmed. It might be quite amusing. Well, for me, anyway. *You* can no longer get drunk."

"Wait, what?" I turned to Uncle Phil, who was nodding. "I can't get tipsy anymore?"

"I would've thought the bulletproof aspect would've been more interesting to you, but no, you cannot get tipsy anymore," Uncle Phil told me. "That would be dangerous for you and for the Magical Midway, considering the power you now hold. So it's not allowed."

"This is starting to sound less fun," I told him.

"You're right, Charlotte. Incredible cosmic superpowers are simply not worth the trade-off of no longer being able to get giddy on champagne." Fiona rolled her eyes. "You have nearly *unlimited* power. You're almost completely indestructible. Quit complaining."

"If I'm so indestructible, how are you dead, Uncle Phil?"

"I still don't know. I don't see that it matters much. I am dead. Knowing how is not going to change anything."

"He couldn't be killed by magic, and he can't be killed by force, so I think your uncle had to have been poisoned," Fiona opined as we walked toward Hildegaard's kitchen. "Ringmasters can commit suicide, and the few that have chosen, themselves, to move on did it by poisoning themselves. That's the only thing I can think of."

"But Uncle Phil would've had to give it to himself, right?"

"Yes, because that technically would've made it self-inflicted."

"That seems like one hell of a loophole."

"No magic is perfect, your highness," Fiona pointed out. "There's *always* a loophole."

"How do you know all this?" I asked Fiona as we walked.

"Circus School. This is pretty basic history. *Everyone* knows this stuff."

"Well, I don't."

"Everyone knows that, too."

Stupendous.

As we walked into Hildegaard's, all conversations stopped along with any laughing, horseplay, and joviality. Cautious eyes stared back at me from every corner of the tent. Heads tipped in my direction with silent respect for the role I now held, while each considered my new place in that role thoughtfully.

"Good morning!" I called cheerfully to the assembled paranormals. A low murmur responded to acknowledge my greeting. "Please, don't stop your conversations on my account." Whispered murmuring filled the tent as the forty or so paranormals leaned into one another.

"Great job, oh powerful leader," Fiona commented sarcastically.

"Really?"

"No. No, not really," Fiona said as she covered her face with her hands and sighed. Turning, she continued. "A speech would have been a good idea here. You only come here for one week a year, Charlotte. Most of these people don't really know you. And you don't know them."

"Tell your friend there will be time for that later," Uncle Phil said. "Right now, you know less than you should. Much, much less. Any speech you make will no doubt make that clear and only make those who depend on you more nervous. I suggest meeting everyone individually, so every group feels respected. There will be time for speeches later, my girl."

"Okay, sounds like a good idea," I answered, and relayed Uncle Phil's advice to Fiona. With a grudging sigh, she agreed.

"You'll want to get as much done as you can before the Council shows up, anyway," Fiona pointed out.

"The Witches' Council? I thought they just governed towns?"

"Let's not worry about them for the moment," Uncle Phil said as he hovered beside us. "We need to talk to the lares first."

"The Larry brothers? The guys that do security?"

"Oh, this is where I leave you." Fiona stepped away. "Those guys are creepy, and talking to you while you are talking to your uncle is confusing. I need to talk to Doug anyway and let him know that you woke up. Though I suppose he figured that out based on the sunshine."

"I'll see you later, Fiona." I watched my friend skip away toward the kelpies tent as she waved.

"The lares can be a little intimidating, Charlotte, but they are sworn to protect the Midway. It's a good idea for you to make sure that you keep the lines of communication open with them," Uncle Phil related as he floated beside me.

We made our way past the rides, pens, and games toward the Magical Midway Security Station.

～

"Ringmaster," the four Larry brothers said as they snapped to attention. Gallus, Lucius, Marcius, and Julius Larry stood straight and tall in a precision line against the south wall of the security station.

"Hey, yo, Charlotte!" Bob Larry called from his perch atop the counter. "Thrilling trip back to the land of the sunshine! I didn't feel, like, a single bump or anything. Score!" He threw his arms up to mimic a goalpost.

I glanced at the four Roman guards staring into space with implacable faces and turned back to the fifth Roman guard casually draped across the dividing ledge between the front and back of the station. Bob's uniform was wrinkled and untucked as he bit into a red apple and dribbled juice across the front of his shirt.

"Bob is…special," my uncle confided.

"Special as in…?"

"Not what you would expect from lares guards," Uncle Phil continued. "Gallus, Lucius, Marcius, and Julius are all typical lares. Bob has chosen to explore a more…the modern side of his personality."

"You talkin' to your uncle? He telling you about what a star Lar I am? Get it? *Star Lar*? Aw, man, I crack myself up," Bob hit the counter as he laughed uproariously at his own joke. I raised my eyebrow.

"Aren't lares supposed to be very serious and intimidating and all that?"

"Yes," the four severe Larry brothers barked out without moving a muscle.

"Hey, now! We all get to choose who we want to be. I learned that at 'The Best Better You' seminar I took once at a hotel in Rhode Island. Changed my life for just $995! I *choose* to be happy because if I'm not going to make myself happy, who's gonna do it for me? Am I right? Of *course,* I'm right," Bob nodded and took another bite out of his apple, dribbling more juice down the front of his uniform.

"Um. Stellar," I answered. I glanced back at my uncle and then turned to the five brothers. "So you guys are like the police force of the Midway?"

"Yes," the four severe Larry brothers barked out.

"Kinda. We're, like, all-around protection. We protect people, places, roads, lakes. We can protect trees. Houses. Yurts. You want it protected, we can protect it. We can protect events, too! We also make *delicious* Italian food from scratch," Bob told me proudly.

"So, who is in charge of the investigation?"

The Larry brothers glanced at each other in confusion.

"Like, after a crime is committed, which one of you guys is the one who would go look into how that crime was committed and catch the perpetrator?"

"We protect things," Bob repeated again slowly as if I had not understood him the first time. "If something wasn't protected, that's just, like, *life*, man. Gotta accept things and move forward from them, ya know? Always something else to protect."

"I get that. Really, I do. What I am trying to understand is who investigates crimes? Like my uncle's murder?"

The Larry brothers glanced at each other again in confusion as if I was speaking a foreign language.

"Maybe, like, the fortune teller could do that?" Bob asked hopefully. I stared at him and waited for him to laugh at the joke, but he didn't.

"Is there any other law enforcement besides you guys at the Magical Midway?"

"Yes," Julius Larry nodded once.

"You," Marcius Larry told me.

CHAPTER 4

"So, I'm the head investigator and judge and cop and everything?" I asked the shimmering ghost of my smiling uncle when we were back in his yurt. "I don't have any experience investigating a murder!"

"You don't have any experience with anything in the Magical Midway other than walking through it and looking pretty, my girl," Uncle Phil pointed out as he hovered over the bed. Uncle Phil's smile continued full and amused with no particular indication of concern.

It figures.

What did he have to worry about? He's dead. He doesn't have to deal with these problems anymore other than as an ephemeral observer and magical Dear Abby.

"Why are you sitting on the bed? Can you even sit as a ghost?"

"Habit, my dear girl," Uncle Phil said as he patted the area next to him. "Come sit next to me and let's talk about this. You look like you might faint."

I paced back and forth in the center of the room, pausing periodically to glare skeptically at my uncle. The confidence I felt about taking over the Magical Midway had all but disappeared in the morning light. I mean, Fiona knew more about my role from paranormal elementary school than I did. That wasn't inspiring self-confidence.

I wondered whether the feeling I could handle this when we were standing in the bubble was my own, or if it had been some side effect of the magic that transferred my uncle's considerable power. As the tingling of the magical energy settled within my body, my unease rose.

"Stop patting the bed like you're actually touching anything. Pacing back and forth works just fine for me at the moment, thank you very much," I said. Uncle Phil smiled and waited for me to get my fidgety panic attack under control.

I told you that you should have chosen her father, Samson thought toward my uncle.

"Are you supposed to be *my* familiar now? Doesn't support and help come with that?" I asked the cat.

Emotional support is not on my list of obligations, no, Samson answered. *Had supporting Astleys emotionally been on my list of familiar commitments, I likely would have found the nearest werewolf and asked him to eat me a long time ago.*

"Charlotte, if you couldn't do this, the power would not have passed to you," Uncle Phil said as his sunny smile faded and his expression turned more serious. "I have been where you are. I do understand how overwhelming this is, and I promise you that we can get through it together."

"Uncle Phil, we still don't know who killed you. That means we don't know *why* someone killed you. You could have been poisoned because you did something to somebody and they were angry. You also could have been killed because you were the ringmaster, and someone wanted the ringmaster dead," I told him as my pacing slowed.

"Well, yes, those could both be possibilities, my girl," Uncle Phil agreed. "But I'm dead now. So whatever reason someone wanted me killed, they achieved their objective. I don't see why we need to waste time on the whys and wherefores of the situation. We need to get you more familiar with your role as the ringmaster. That is much more important than figuring out the end of my silly little story."

"But now *I'm* the ringmaster. So if someone wanted *you* dead because *you* were the ringmaster, they might try to kill *me*. And no one's even looking into it."

Uncle Phil stared at me as if he had swallowed a leprechaun.

"Oh, I see what you mean," Uncle Phil said quietly. Then his face brightened, and he snapped his fingers. "Well, don't eat or drink anything, my girl, and you should be fine."

"You're a ghost! *You* don't have to drink or eat to survive, but I'm still human. I still have to eat." As I pointed this out to Uncle Phil, my stomach growled loudly. I realized that I had not eaten in two days, and it was lunchtime.

You are not human, Samson pointed out as he slumbered on the bed next to Uncle Phil. *You are a witch. A witch is not human. A human cannot be a witch.*

"Slow your roll there, Samson. Since I am a

witch does that mean I don't need to eat or drink to survive?"

Of course not. You still need nourishment like any other living thing.

"Well, why did you bother pointing that out?"

One thing I must do is correct your ignorance.

"Oh, man, this is going to take every ounce of patience that I have," I grumbled.

Likewise, said Samson.

"We will have to deal with the food and drink situation later. At the moment, I think we need to discuss what we're going to tell the Witches' Council," Uncle Phil said. "I have no doubt that they'll be here within the next couple of hours."

"What do they have to do with the Magical Midway?"

The Witches' Council consists of the governing body for all witches on the planet and witches in directly accessible paranormal alternate realms adjacent to our primary reality, Samson informed me. *All witches are subject to their guidelines and judgment.*

"Well, within their power to enforce the judgment," Uncle Phil chuckled.

True. The Council has incredible power over witches. No one can hide from them, and few can get away with anything for long. There are, however, two witches that possess a power even more significant than the Council's.

"And they are?"

The two ringmasters of the last two surviving paranormal circuses. That would be you and Roland Makepeace. Roland is your counterpart at the Makepeace Circus.

Samson's eyes were closed as he lay curled up on the bed. His tail flipped back and forth lazily. Though we were conversing, you would never know it from looking at the black cat.

"So, what does that mean, exactly? Break it down for me in practical terms."

"It means they don't like you very much, Charlotte," Uncle Phil warned.

They hate you, Samson countered bluntly. *They believe no witch should have more power than the Council. While outwardly they make a show of supporting the objectives of both circuses, internally they do not. A few have secretly been working on getting rid of all the carnivals. They want to take their magic.*

This whole ringmaster thing just keeps getting better and better.

"So why are they coming here?"

"They always show up when the power's first passed. I got my first visit from the Council within twenty-four hours," Uncle Phil said. "They'll probably send the three witches from the Ministry, so that would be Mina, Mabel, and Mercy. They'll act all authoritarian and will hope that you don't realize you really don't need to listen to them."

Once they realize you know that what they demand means less to you than a wand in the teeth of a rabbit, their personalities will become decidedly less friendly, Samson added.

"Fantastic. Do I have anything to worry about, you know, physically? Are they going to attack me or beat me up or cast some crazy spell in my direction?"

"No, nothing like that," Uncle Phil assured me. "Witches are not allowed to harm other witches, even if you could be harmed that way. In fact, no paranormal is allowed to harm another paranormal."

"And everyone abides by that?"

"Of *course* not!" my uncle laughed. "Your defenses, however, will work on anything they throw at you. Oh my stars, it really gets their goat, too."

My uncle's ghostly body shook with laughter as I glared at him.

The Council will abide, Samson said. *They are*

the law-bearers of your kind. Should any of the Witches' Council harm a witch, the scandal would be an enormous one. It would undermine their power, and if there is one thing the Witches' Council would never do it's anything that would undermine their power.

As the three of us spoke, a hush seemed to fall outside of the yurt. The Magical Midway always bustled with some activity if the sun was up. There were stands to be mended, foods to fix, and coats to brush continuously. The dull murmur of over a hundred paranormals chatting and going about their daily chores was a constant soundtrack on the fairgrounds.

That noise had all but disappeared.

"They must be here," Uncle Phil told me quickly. "They know you can contact me, but they do not know that the ringmasters have near-constant contact with their predecessors. Let's not tell them."

I nodded and swallowed nervously.

You will do fine, Samson said with confidence. The cat lifted his head from his paws and stared into my eyes. *After all, over one hundred paranormals are depending on you. There is no option to do other than fine.*

I stared at the slit that served as the entrance

and exit to Uncle Phil's yurt and waited. I
wondered what other surprises were in store for
me I did not know were coming—and that I
would no doubt be woefully unprepared for.

Bob Larry stuck his scruffy head in the opening
and swept his eyes around the tent. It occurred to
me that Bob didn't realize Uncle Phil was in the
room. From his viewpoint, his new boss was
standing in an empty tent while a cat slept quietly
on the bed. I made a mental note to ask Uncle
Phil who knew what about the power we had and
the things we could do, after the meeting with the
Witches' Council.

"Hey, boss lady?" Bob called after nosily
examining the entire interior with quickly
scanning eyes. "There are three witches here to
see you from some Council. You want me to
make them go away?"

"No, Bob, go ahead and show them in, please,"
I told him as my uncle shimmered and
disappeared. "Wait! Where you going?"

Bob tilted his head and stared at me. "Um. To
go get them. Like you just told me?"

"I'm sorry, Bob, go ahead." Bob eased slowly

out of the tent backward while his eyes were glued to me.

I am still here, Uncle Phil's voice echoed in my mind. *It's distracting to have my visual presence in front of you, so I just made myself invisible for the meeting. Don't worry, Charlotte. I can still see and hear everything. Be careful. Just think* to *me, niece.*

I feel like I will never get the hang of this, I thought forcefully.

You will, he sent back. *Everyone feels overwhelmed at the beginning. You are doing fine, Charlotte. Samson and I are right here.*

At that moment, the yurt flaps parted wide and pushed out well into the circled room. In a line, three women walked in one after another, their faces pursed as if each had sucked a lemon, and all held their arms against their bodies tightly to avoid touching anything. The energy of haughty judgment surrounded them like a mean-girl aura.

They stopped in a chorus line before me with broad smiles as their teeth sparkled. Their eyes narrowed as they weighed me.

"Charlotte Astley!" boomed the redheaded woman who had been the first to enter. I flinched at the painfully loud volume. Her flaming hair was piled high atop her slender head and tumbled from an updo that would be more appropriate at prom than a circus.

"Congratulations! We of the World Council of Witches extend our most sincere and most affectionate hand toward the newest witch leader of our magical world!" The redhead stuck her hand straight out from her body nearly poking me in the chest. As I shook it firmly, she continued. "I am Mina World, Chairwoman of the Ministry for Peace and Understanding."

"P.U. for short," the platinum blonde standing next to her cooed with an even broader smile as I struggled not to burst out laughing.

Despite the name, these three are the heads of the committee that deals with propaganda, persuasion, internal civility, and human/witch relations, Uncle Phil sent. *Mainly, they try to tell everybody how to think and how to act.*

"Thank you so much," I told Mina as I pulled my hand back. "Can I get you ladies something to drink or eat?"

"*Surely* not," the brunette snapped. "I *certainly* don't want to ingest the same witch killing poison that cut your uncle down."

"How did you know that my Uncle Phil was poisoned?" I asked the brunette sharply. Her eyes grew wide, and she turned her head away to break my gaze. The other two witches snapped their heads around to stare at her.

"The WCW tries to make sure that it knows *everything* that goes on in the territories that we are responsible for overseeing. Which is everywhere, of course," Mina said as she turned back to me. "Mabel is simply exercising due care for her person, considering this location was the scene of a tragic witch murder not twenty-four hours ago."

Wow. Time really had stopped when we were...well, wherever we were.

"Of course," I answered noncommittally and smiled at the sour Mabel.

"It must be so *terrible* to be in charge of such a dirty place and so cut off from your *own kind*," Mercy said breathlessly as she stepped toward me like we were lifelong best friends. "Just the smell of this place would be enough to make me *run* for the hills if I didn't have to be here. *Animal* paranormals, and not another witch for *miles*. What a *travesty*."

"Not at all," I responded calmly. "I grew up living on a property that doubled as an animal shelter, so this is all pretty normal to me."

"An animal shelter? Like real, mundane, smelly animals?"

Are all witches like this? I thought toward my uncle.

No, he responded. *These three are a particularly uppity breed of witch. Just like in the human world, it seems the narcissistic jerks always rise. No doubt because good people rarely entertain a desire to control everyone else, while narcissistic jerks chase that ambition like a weregreyhound after a rabbit.*

"Yes, my parents still run it. They've saved thousands of homeless pets over the years. It was really a fantastic way to grow up. In fact, the Magical Midway contributes a significant portion of the operating expenses to that shelter and saving those animals."

"Now, ladies, it takes all kinds in the witch world, and we *certainly* don't *look down* on any *witch*, do we?" Mina said to the other two women in a tone that was both sickly sweet and razor-sharp all at once.

"No, Mina," Mercy and Mabel answered simultaneously as they shook their heads. A quick sampling of each woman's sincerity clued me in to what a monstrous fib that was. Not that I needed magic to figure that out.

"Well, I want to thank you for stopping by, but this is my first day on the job, and I have so many things I need to do. Is there anything else that you need before I get back to work?"

"Oh, dear me, Charlotte," Mina said as she rolled her eyes. "We were just starting out with pleasant and friendly formalities to make you feel at ease. I thought *that* would be *obvious*. Wasn't that *obvious*, ladies?" Mina said as she glowered to Mercy and Mabel demanding support. The two women flanking the redhead nodded emphatically as they agreed with their leader.

"Doesn't change the fact that I have a lot to do, so let's get on with why you're here." Though I tried to ensure my tone was amicable, my impatience with their false friendliness was rising.

"Well, that was *rude*," Mabel mumbled. I sighed and waited.

"We just wanted to ensure that we got the membership contract signed by the new ringmaster," Mina said as she pulled out a rolled up parchment with a flourish. "*Simply* a formality, of course, but you understand the *necessity* for paperwork in a bureaucracy such as the WCW. It protects you and the Midway, of course." Mina's minions nodded in agreement.

"Of course," I agreed flatly as I took the parchment from her and unrolled it.

This is unnecessary, Uncle Phil told me. *We are witches, Charlotte. We don't have membership contracts, we have magical oaths and pacts. I never had to sign anything.*

I held the parchment up far enough away from me I hoped Uncle Phil could read it while I skimmed over its contents. The parchment was written in ink that had barely dried. After scanning three or four of the agreements laid out on the fancy paper, I understood the gist of what the three women had traveled here trying to achieve.

So if I sign this, the WCW has full control over the Magical Midway, and my magical powers are limited to only acting as the anchor of the Midway? I lose all defensive spells, all offensive spells, all travel spells, everything?

That's what it looks like to me, Uncle Phil concurred. *By signing this, you would cede Astley family control to the WCW for the Midway. They would also take Samson.*

Pardon me, they would take who now? The cat's voice suddenly sprang into the center of the conversation as Samson's head raised an alert on the bed and stared at the three women. The aura around him glowed a dark red. I wondered if the three women could see it.

"Do you need a pen, dear?" Mina asked me sweetly holding out a feather and inkwell. Suddenly the parchment in my hand burst into flames. In seconds, it was a pile of ash on the ground between the three witches and me.

What happened? I thought.

You're lucky all I did was turn that contract to ash. I briefly contemplated stabbing her in the eye with that feather, Samson's voice echoed as his red aura dissipated.

"She's a silent one of action," Mabel said to the other two women. "This one will be a problem."

"Oh, they've *all* been *problems*, Mabel," Mina snapped. The coquettishly blonde Mercy stared at me in awe. "Even though they have *all* been problems, we have brought the nomads down from thirty-seven groups to just two."

"I don't know anything about the other groups," I told Mina as I stepped closer to her. "But I do know who I am, and the Magical Midway is mine now. I don't know what you did to all the other ringmasters, but I can tell you one thing. You're not going to do it to me."

"The middle way of anything never accomplished much, you foolish girl," Mabel said as her eyes glowed. "A witch that lives among the homeless dregs of the lowest paranormals.

Offense! A witch that allows humans within paranormal land! Injustice! No witch should have as much power as you ringmasters do. You are rogues, rebels, and outcasts. And your time is almost up."

"Yeah, maybe. But not quite yet."

I stared at the three women and thought *Go Home*. They instantly disappeared as the feather and inkwell dropped to the ground.

"Charlotte, are you all right?" Fiona asked as she walked swiftly into the tent. She gazed around as if expecting to see upturned furniture and things on fire, sighing with relief as she realized both I and the tent were intact. "I felt the three furies leave."

"Wait a minute, those three were furies, too? Like witch furies?"

"No, no, they're just witches. I just call them the three furies because of their winning personalities. How did your first meeting with them go?"

"Well, they tried to get me to sign a contract to give up the Magical Midway, Samson set the contract on fire, and then I magically blinked them back to wherever they came from without asking their permission. So, all in all, I'm going to rate the meeting as 'not good.' They really, really don't seem to like us."

"Oh, they like *you* just fine," Fiona chirped as she bounced on the bed and sat cross-legged next to Samson. "It's us *lesser* paranormals they don't like. They like it when the WCW is in charge of dictating everything for all paranormals. They act as if witches are the only paranormals that matter and expect all witches to act accordingly. Give them that, and they are sweet as pie."

"Authoritarian, elitist, bigoted witches? Outstanding."

Uncle Phil shimmered into view and clapped his ghost hands together. Creepily, that act didn't make a sound.

You did splendid, my girl! Simply splendid! It was surprisingly enjoyable watching you give those dour, judgmental women what for!

"One thing really bothers me about the meeting, though, Uncle Phil," I told him as I sat down in the chair near my uncle's old writing desk.

Just one thing?

"*How* did they know that you had died of poison? Is there some magical spell or crystal ball or something that they could have looked into that would've given them that information?"

Only if one of them had psychometry as a talent, and at that only if they had an object of mine that was in my possession at the time of the poisoning. I'm not even sure the Council would be able to do so then. The Midway is quite shielded, he told me.

"Those harpies knew that Phil had been poisoned?" Fiona asked.

"Yes, and Uncle Phil just told me there's only one way they may have known it magically, and he's not even sure that would have actually worked."

"So, they either knew it through magic, or they know it because somebody told them."

"Not just somebody. The killer," I told Fiona.

"How do you figure that?"

"Last night during the ceremony, my father said publicly that Uncle Phil was murdered. No one said *anything* about poison. Only those of us in this room and my Dad know that's what we suspect. Fiona, how did you know about the defensive abilities I inherited when my uncle passed the ringmaster role to me?"

"I told you, Circus School. Well, some of it was from Circus School. All of my kind can sense the abilities of witches. I suspect this was an evolutionary thing that developed during the thousands of years kelpies and witches were enemies. If we could sense you, we could avoid you."

"Do you guys share that information with anyone? What you sense in certain witches?"

"Ay, no. Why would we? It's *our* talent, right? If you weren't the ringmaster, I wouldn't be telling *you*."

"This whole paranormal species thing is way more complicated than I expected it would be," I mumbled. I reached for the glass sitting on my uncle's writing table and brought it toward my lips.

No! Samson and my uncle shouted in my mind as Fiona leaped from the bed and forcefully knocked the glass out of my hand before it reached my lips. The glass flew across the tent and shattered against the wall just above my uncle's potted herb garden. Drops of liquid sprayed the tiny plants below.

We all watched in horror as each herb withered, blackened, and died.

CHAPTER 5

UNCLE PHIL, FIONA, SAMSON AND I WERE relieved that the death of the herb plants had taken place instead of the end of *me*. A quick check with my uncle confirmed that the cup had been sitting on his desk since the night he died. The container contained his daily magical sleeping-draft, an elixir Uncle Phil downed nightly after his evening constitutional. As far as he could remember, the cup was waiting on his writing desk as it always was.

"Who normally prepares the cup, Uncle Phil?"

Jeannie from Jeannie's Snack Shop. She's been preparing it for me for over two years now. Every night.

"Would she have any reason to hurt you or want you dead?"

I should think not! Uncle Phil boomed as little red fireworks sparked around the image of the body he used to have. *Jeannie positively adores me!*

"Who got him the drink?" Fiona asked as she tried to keep up with the conversation by following my side.

"Jeannie from the snack shop?"

"She's an awfully lovely genie. I just can't see her poisoning anyone, though she would have the ability. I wonder if your uncle did something manlike to hurt her feelings. While she's a nice lady, dating a djinn can be a dangerous thing when you tick them off."

"Wait, she *is* a genie or her name is Jeannie?"

"Both. She was also your uncle's girlfriend."

Uncle Phil squinted up at the ceiling and began silently whistling. With no air, he just appeared kind of silly.

"Okay, wait, let's back up a second. Fiona, you said that you and the other kelpies could sense additional witches when they come onto the Magical Midway. On the night Uncle Phil was killed, did you sense anyone at the Midway? Before we start looking at other people, I'd like to figure out if there's any possibility the WCW killed my uncle."

"I did not, and none of the other kelpies mention sensing anything other than Phil's death. We felt the distinct sudden absence of *any* witch on the grounds."

"So the WCW couldn't have sent someone here to kill Uncle Phil."

That's not necessarily the case, Uncle Phil said, and I held up a hand to silence Fiona so I could hear him. *We are dealing with powerful witches. Just because the kelpies can sense a witch under normal circumstances does not mean that the Witches' Council didn't have a magical means to block the kelpies. The Council is aware of what magical creatures live and travel with the Magical Midway through the Paranormal Census. If they had tried to off me, they could have utilized magical means to hide from discovery. They have much knowledge we do not. They could know about the kelpies' ability.*

I repeated Uncle Phil's observation to Fiona, and she reluctantly agreed that while it was likely the kelpies would've sensed a witch, it was not impossible that their senses could have been blocked.

"So, it could have been the WCW, but the kelpies would've sensed them, but the kelpies may not have sensed them if they were using magic. The drink was prepared by Jeannie, so Jeannie had the opportunity to put poison in the cup for Uncle Phil to drink," I told them both. "We have two suspects at this point."

Three, Samson interjected. *I turned to the cat. That quiet mentalist man from the Langdon Circus. I saw him near this tent that night.*

"Why didn't you say anything?"

My job is to prevent catastrophes. Once the calamity has taken place, I don't need to worry about it anymore, do I?

"I swear, this whole place and everyone in it has a *bizarre* aversion to examining how something happened."

Samson lifted his head open his eyes and turned his sharp gaze to me. With his eyes narrowing he said, *No place is perfect.* The small black cat laid his head back down on his paws and sighed.

"Who is the mentalist?" I asked Uncle Phil and Fiona.

He is actually a telepath, a human one. His name is Mark Botsworth. He came to us looking for a place after the Langdon Circus closed down. He seemed a pleasant enough fellow, and Chloe Langdon spoke highly of him when I called her for a reference, Uncle Phil said.

"Paranormals get references?"

"Yes, but even with them he gives me the creeps," Fiona told me. I raised my eyebrow. "He slinks around the Midway. Doesn't talk to anyone, doesn't seem to have any friends."

Mark cannot read the minds of paranormals, Uncle Phil told me as I turned toward him and away from Fiona. *I imagine that for a human that can read other human minds, living here and getting to know new people that you can't read must be challenging for him.*

I sat down on the bed and thought about the various suspects in situations surrounding Uncle Phil in the Magical Midway. Everything seemed like a possibility, and yet nothing jumped out at me as the answer.

The Witches' Council seemed like the most likely suspect, though admittedly I suspected them because they were jerks. Had they killed Uncle Phil, though, would they have shown up here the next day?

It seemed like quite a risk to step onto the Midway and be so openly hostile to a ringmaster just a day after the murder of one.

On the other hand, if the Council was the law

and they broke the law…Was there anyone that would hold them to account?

With three suspects already and over a hundred paranormals and humans calling the Magical Midway home, this would not be easy to figure out.

I had to unravel it, though. And fast.

It was lunchtime, and I was getting hungry.

The three of us left Uncle Phil's yurt and stepped out into the late morning sunlight while Samson remained behind to snooze. I could not believe that only twelve regular hours had passed since I had been teleported to this clearing.

The private yurts were set up in the southwestern corner of the Magical Midway tucked behind several carnival games. It was called the backyard in carnival lingo, an area of the grounds that patrons could not visit, with all the residential areas like yurts and food tents.

The northern entry point was squeezed behind the carousel, and the southern entry point right behind the security station. To the west of the yurts was a football field of space with a shimmering border at the edge that only paranormals could see. This boundary encircled the Midway like a dome and protected all of its inhabitants from both harm and human discovery.

A human standing outside the boundary could look toward the Magical Midway and see nothing that would cause him or her alarm or concern. If a paranormal stood outside the perimeter and checked out the Midway, they would know without a doubt they had found others of their kind.

The magic that protected this place and enabled it to move was complicated, and I didn't understand it yet. I knew that these things—the shimmering boundary that obfuscated what we were, the paranormals' yurts that were bigger on the inside, the power to lift and instantly relocate the entire Magical Midway—were now anchored somehow within me.

Any of these paranormals could have left the Magical Midway at any time and taken up residence in one of a couple dozen paranormal towns, but they didn't. I knew that many people had been here with my family for generations. Fiona's family had been part of the Magical Midway since the late 1800s, performing an enchanting and awe-inspiring horse show.

With only two paranormal traveling fairs left, those that preferred this nomadic lifestyle had few options. They now depended on me to safeguard their home and their way of life. A way of life I barely understood.

No pressure.

Kat Riddle fixed her eyes on us as we passed between her *Guess Your Weight* game and the *Milk Bottle* game on our way to Jeannie's Snack Shop. The golden blonde woman with the striking metallic eyes lifted her hand and waved us over. I waved back and kept walking.

You have to stop, niece, Uncle Phil told me as I sighed with impatience. *You are the new ringmaster, and many will want to connect with you. Especially those who do not already know you well. It's part of the job, dear girl.*

"Hello, Charlotte Astley, the great circus heir," Kat called almost musically as she grabbed my two hands. "I welcome our new leader to this paranormal fair! I am so sorry about your Uncle Phil's demise, but I am sure in choosing you he was nothing but wise."

"I…um…thank you," I sputtered as the woman's rhymes confused me. "I don't think we've ever formally met before. If it's not too rude of me, what type of paranormal creature are you?"

"Why, I am a sphinx, of which there are few. Here at the Midway, I am but one of two. My husband Ari also lives in this place, but he left to get ice cream instead of cleaning our space," Kat told me with some frustration as she waived her cleaning rag in front of her. "I would love to move our stand away from temptation before my dear husband becomes more aggravation."

"I thought sphinxes only spoke in riddles?"

"We have evolved over time to speak answers that rhyme." Kat smiled and squeezed my hands. "I do not wish to take up too much of your time."

"No, it's no problem at all. I want to meet and get to know everyone here. It just may take me a while."

"I just wanted you to know we welcome this new paradigm. Come by for dinner soon! We have wonderful wine," the golden woman nodded as she gave a little bow and stepped back up to her Midway game.

Once we were far enough away that Kat Riddle couldn't overhear, I asked Fiona if Kat and her husband *always* talked like that. Fiona confirmed that every conversation with the sphinxes involved riddles or rhymes, and I was lucky that I got no riddle.

"If they decide to fling a riddle at ya, just *run*. Trust me. If you get far enough away from whichever Sphinx is doin' the riddlin' before they get to the end of the riddle, you don't feel compelled to solve it," Fiona advised.

Good to know.

As we continued on our way, I hoped that I wouldn't have any need to interview Kat or her husband about my uncle's murder. I might need to take a preemptive aspirin just to get through it.

We crossed the main corridor of the Magical Midway, and I spotted Jeannie's Snack Shop just a few feet away. The windows were shuttered, and the interior of the small yellow building was dark. We walked around toward the back and knocked on the door to see if anyone was inside.

Minutes later, an older woman, a brunette with shocks of gray in her messy hair, peeked out through the crack of the slowly opening door. I could hear the sniffling before she spoke, but once her raspy voice answered there could be no doubt she had been crying. "Yes?"

"Hi, Jeannie? You might remember me, I'm Charlotte Astley, Phil Astley's niece."

At the mention of Uncle Phil's name, Jeannie

wailed. She flung the door open in a grief-stricken version of a welcome and covered her face with her hands as she turned her back and shuffled back inside.

Oh, that poor, poor dear, Uncle Phil said as he watched her disappear into the darkness. *Now, Charlotte, you be kind to that woman. I know that you have some suspicions that she murdered me or some such nonsense, but I cared about her very much. Don't you go all gangbusters on her, dear girl. I will be quite put out with you.*

Uncle Phil, just because you cared about her doesn't mean she cared about you. I'm just trying to cover all the bases. You were poisoned by her *drink,* I thought to my uncle.

Poppycock, Uncle Phil grumbled. *That woman wouldn't hurt a fly. In fact, she traps flies and releases them over by the were-elephant enclosure.*

I'm sure you're right. Let's make sure.

Fiona and I stepped up into the snack shop and closed the door gently behind us. The interior of the shop was dark, and though some fans were circulating air, the building felt stifling and stuffy. It was as if Jeannie's tears had escalated the humidity beyond what the small space could comfortably tolerate.

Jeannie hunched back toward a chair that

leaned against what I assumed was her cooking counter. On the stand, a single white candle burned next to one pink and one purple rose.

"I am sorry," Jeannie sniffled as she sat down turned in our direction. "I just loved your uncle so very much. He was a very kind man and a lovely boyfriend. On the night that he died, he took me on a boat ride under the full moon. He was so romantic…" Jeannie coughed and sniffled, but her tears grew thicker as they dripped down her sad face.

"Did you leave the Midway that night? Where was this boat ride?"

"No, we stayed at the Midway. We were all alone on the Charybdis Boat Ride, and he made sparkling colors in the water just for me. All pink and purple roses. Such a dear, dear man," she cried.

You see? There's no way she could've killed me, Uncle Phil pronounced with finality.

Why? Because she's telling me what a remarkable man you are?

Well, yes. You don't kill someone that you like. Why would anyone kill someone that made flowers of light in the water on a boat ride? That would be preposterous! Uncle Phil exclaimed.

I sighed and closed my eyes. All the

complaints my father had over the years about paranormals and their disconnect from reality came into perfect clarity. These people didn't just live in a different world. These people lived in a lollipop and cotton candy world where everyone was honest, and nothing terrible ever happened to anyone. If something terrible happened? Just move on from it. It was like it never happened.

Granted, the Witches' Council didn't seem to have this worldview.

Perhaps it was just circus people that were utterly naïve and total idiots about human...er, paranormal nature. Maybe all the death-defying tricks that everyone did created some filter bubble of positivity that permeated these people's brains.

I stopped myself.

I knew it was just frustration, and I wasn't being entirely fair. Jeannie also clearly hadn't moved on from it. She was visibly grieving over losing Uncle Phil, and while I sensed it was genuine, I didn't think her grief meant she had no answers. I pushed, but as gently as I could.

"Jeannie, did you prepare Uncle Phil's sleepy-time drink that night?"

Sleepy-time drink? What am I, twelve? Uncle Phil asked, offended.

Be quiet. I need to listen.

Jeannie rubbed her eyes with a dish towel and nodded as Fiona stood beside the woman and rubbed her back. "I made it for him every night. It was just easier for me to do it than for Hildegaard to do it. The ingredients were so specific, and I didn't need to use them."

"What do you mean? How do you make something without ingredients?"

"I am a djinn. Nothing that I make here at the snack shop is actually *made*. I simply grant your wishes. Someone comes to my counter and wishes for a specific food or drink, and I grant their wish. Well, technically, I *sell* them their wish. For a modest price."

"Can genies actually *sell* wishes? I mean, is that legal? Doesn't it violate some wish-granting ethic or something?"

Jeannie's eyes narrowed dangerously, and I quickly changed the subject.

"Sorry, off-topic. So, you just granted my uncle's wish each night and manifested his sleepy-time drink magically?"

Stop calling it that! It's an evening draft. It's a slumber potion. It's a restful refreshment. It's a lullaby libation. It is not a sleepy-time drink! Uncle Phil protested vehemently.

I told you to hush.

"Yes, though I liked to think the drink was *my* wish. If I could have made a wish to myself, I would have wished to ensure that Phil had a wonderful sleep and would wake cheerful and happy in the morning," Jeannie said. Suddenly, her head snapped up, and she eyed me suspiciously. "Why are you asking me all these questions about his sleepy-time drink?"

Now you have her doing it! Uncle Phil bellowed while waving his arms.

"Charlotte is just asking because it seems that her uncle's sleepy time drink was the thing that poisoned him," Fiona told her softly as she continued slowly rubbing the genie's back.

"That's *impossible!*" Jeannie shouted as her face fell in horror. "I had the exact ingredients! I wished for those exact ingredients! There was nothing in the sleepy time drink that shouldn't have been in there!"

"Is there any possibility at all that the wish could've gone wrong?" I held my hands up before Jeannie could take offense to my suggestion. "I mean *any* kind of possibility. You were sick, or you had a headache, or you had drunk a little bit earlier in the evening, and perhaps your mind was slightly clouded. Is there any possibility whatsoever that the drink you manifested could have accidentally had poison in it?"

"None," she insisted. "Genies *cannot* cause harm with our powers. It's a limitation on our wish granting ability. We can *only* do good and make people happy. Nothing in our magic is capable of being destructive. If I even tried to harm another, I would wish myself out of existence."

"Wow, that's a pretty harsh penalty. What if you're attacked, or someone threatens you? You still can't use your magic to harm another? Even if it's to protect yourself?" I asked her.

"No, not even then," Jeannie told me as she reached beneath the counter and pulled out a shiny black gun. "That's what I have my human-world Ruger for."

Okay, every paranormal isn't wholly naïve and all lollipops and cotton candy. The genie was packing heat.

I thought through all the information I had and tried to figure out some way that poison had got in that cup. It didn't sound like it was possible that Jeannie had manifested it there accidentally, and I sensed nothing but genuine shock and pain from her at the thought her drink killed Uncle Phil.

"Did you bring the cup of sleepy-time to Uncle Phil's tent yourself?"

"No, Dergal brought it over for me. He said he was heading over to a party at the weredeer's tent and offered to bring it with him," Jeannie told me. "The last time I saw the cup that night was when I handed it to him out that window right there."

She pointed to the front counter-service area of the stand. We all stared at it as if it would divulge some secret.

It didn't.

Dergal is a centaur. He is manly. If you call that drink a sleepy-time drink in front of Dergal, I will be quite put out, niece, Uncle Phil threatened.

I thanked Jeannie for talking to us. As we walked out, I heard her sobs begin anew.

For me, Uncle Phil's death represented a transition. He changed from a flesh and blood uncle to an ephemeral representation of the same uncle I had always known. His death represented a massive change in my life, a new role I still wasn't sure I could handle, but he was still with me.

I had to keep reminding myself that for everyone else here, he was gone.

∾

The centaurs' *Ring The Bell* game was just north of *Jeannie's Snack Shop* on the east side of the Midway. Ningul, the leader of the centaurs, gave me a sweaty, muscled hug as I stopped by. Even though kelpies were horse shapeshifters, and centaurs were half horse, half human, the two species didn't resemble one another in their human guise.

Each group's human form seemed to take on a similar style or a body type. For example, the kelpies were lithe and slim and elegant like ballet dancers. The centaurs were muscled and athletic. The Larrys were in-between, well-built but not overly muscled, though each brother sported distinct patrician features that appeared strikingly Roman. The leprechauns were normal-sized but slightly shorter in stature, and all kept their red hair. There were salamanders, and brownies, and naiads. We had a sylph and a yeti. Such a variety existed here; it was hard to remember them all.

Yet even in human form, you could recognize each individual as a member of a distinct tribe within the Magical Midway.

Which brings me back to the centaurs.

Holy horse hooves, they were all *hot*.

The men were sleek and muscled and tall and

powerful, and their voices were masculine and gruff. The women were tall and toned with perfect curves and sharp features. They seemed to be like a biker gang—if that biker gang went to the gym every day, moisturized after every shower, and really, really dressed well.

The male centaurs *always* made me swoon.

As I breathed in Ningul's intoxicating maleness and enjoyed the feel of his perfectly delivered hug, I realized I was the boss now. *I should probably get my drooling attraction to them under control*, I thought as he released me and we asked where Dergal was.

"Dergal is over at the roller coaster today," Ningul said as a breeze blew through his chestnut colored hair. "One of the chains needed repair, and he's the best with his tools."

"Oh, I have no doubt about that," Fiona told Ningul as I fanned myself from the heat of midday. That's what I hoped it looked like, anyway.

Suddenly, Samson's snarky, nosy cat voice broke into my brain's very inappropriate imaginings. *I can hear your thoughts, you know. Even from my very comfortable bed in your yurt. Especially when they're* very loud.

Shut up, Samson.

I'm also standing right next to you, niece, my uncle murmured. *I just didn't want to embarrass you, dear. He is a very handsome young man.*

"Oh my God, we have to go. Thanks!" I told Ningul as I backed away and turned around toward the roller coaster.

"What was that about?" Fiona asked me as she struggled to keep up with my brisk pace away from the embarrassment that was my too-full mind.

"You don't want to know. Trust me. You really, *really* don't want to know."

Never alone. Right.

Got it.

CHAPTER 6

I'D NEVER BEEN GOOD AT MEDITATION.

My mind raced in a thousand directions all the time, and the one meditation class I took in college was an abject failure. There were just too many thoughts, observations, and distractions bouncing around inside my head for me to push them all out. It would have taken a mental bulldozer to shove them all to the side.

Walking the path toward the roller coaster, though, I tried to force the mental contortions needed to lock every fleeting thought, feeling, and idea away from my uncle and the cat that took up seemingly permanent residence in my mind. I supposedly had incredible cosmic power, so surely I could stop my mind from racing like a speed demon kelpie.

"Not going to work," Fiona said as we got closer to the back of the Midway.

"Oh, for goodness sake, can you read my mind now, too? Does everybody in this place have the ability to rummage around inside my head and find out what I'm thinking?"

"I can't read your mind, Charlotte. But the way you're twisting your face up in concentration, it's not hard to figure out what you're trying to do. I wondered how you were going to deal with that aspect of all this."

"Considering how much you know about my supposedly secret abilities, Fiona, why don't you tell me how to block them out?" I snapped at her and then immediately regretted it. I reached out a hand toward my friend and squeezed her arm. "I'm sorry, I didn't mean to gripe at you. This is all just a little overwhelming."

Fiona stopped walking and grabbed my shirt to spin me around. Just looking at my friend, my eyes watered as the stress grew in the fertile confusion that nagged at me. On the one hand, this whole place was ridiculous. On the other hand, this really was all life and death. It was serious, and I was seriously unprepared.

"Now, look here," Fiona said as she stepped closer. "The truth that I know is that no ringmaster is chosen if they cannot handle the job. This place runs in the very blood of your veins, ya ken? You're going to do fine, but you're going to have to start *believing* that you can do it."

"It's hard to believe anything when I'm this hungry and thirsty. I would kidnap a leprechaun for a vanilla milkshake."

"Not to interrupt your whining because, really, I'm fascinated, but Dergal's right over there."

I turned and gazed toward the roller coaster to see yet another hot, sexy, built-like-a-tank centaur walking toward us as if the dirt path were a runway in Paris. We could send the centaurs out to compete with Chippendale's dancers, and they would likely put the humans out of business. Circuses can have male strip shows, right?

No, my uncle thought. *We are family friendly. Male strippers would be utterly offensive. What a shocking thought.*

Well, how do you think families get made, Uncle Phil?

You may want to wipe the drool off the corner of your mouth. It's rather unbecoming for a ringmaster. And stop with those ridiculous ideas.

Oh, get out of my head. I wasn't entertaining the idea seriously. Okay, mostly not seriously.

"Dergal! Over here!" Fiona shouted and waved the centaur over. His eyes scanned the crowd, and for a split second, I could swear I sensed a flash of concern when he spotted us. In the next moment, a broad smile took over and anything I thought I felt was gone. He sexily sauntered over.

"Well, if it isn't the new boss," Dergal crooned as he reached out a powerful hand and caressed my neck, shoulder, and arm.

What the heck?

My innards froze in shock at the intimate gesture. I didn't know Dergal, and I wasn't expecting his hands on me. "What are you two beautiful ladies needing from me? I have *much* to give, you know. I certainly hope you've pulled me aside so that I can be of...*service*."

He winked, and I tried not to retch.

All the attraction I had for Dergal popped like a water balloon. He was a slithery snake or a slimy slug. I couldn't stand guys that used the "*I am so sexy you know you want me*" thing as a come-on. A gentle mist of confidence was attractive in a man. Dergal was trying to spew arrogance all over my personal space like a typhoon.

"We just met with Jeannie, and she mentioned

that you brought Uncle Phil his sleeping drink on the night he died," I told Dergal as I took the measure of his energy in reaction to my statement. While his attractive smile grew wider, his power closed in on itself. Doors snapped shut within his mind, and his strength felt mildly repulsive.

"I don't think it was on that night, no," Dergal answered as he physically stepped closer and fluttered his bedroom eyes in my direction. "I'm *sure* I was back in my tent early that evening. I don't even think I worked that day."

"Wasn't that the night of the weredeer party? Jeannie mentioned that you were going and offered to take the drink over to Uncle Phil for her. His tent is right behind the carousel, so that would make sense. Ring a bell?"

"No, I don't think so," Dergal said sharply, some of his friendliness fading.

"You don't think there was a party, you didn't go if there was a party, or you didn't offer to take the drink?" Dergal's energy pulsed and hummed even stronger repulsiveness at me as he telegraphed a desire to be anywhere other than where he was.

"I really need to get back to Ningul," Dergal said as he stepped back and walked away quickly.

"Sorry I couldn't be of any more help." Fiona and I glared at him as he briskly put as much distance between us as he could without looking more suspicious than he already did.

"I'm not a witch with super psychic abilities or anything, but that seemed just a wee bit concerning, no?" Fiona asked as we stared at Dergal's back.

"He was hiding something," I told her.

"Well, I got *that*, Charlotte," Fiona raised her eyebrow.

Why would Dergal want to kill me? Uncle Phil thought.

Do you remember whether Dergal brought you the drink or not?

No. I just came back to the tent after checking on the weredeer party, and it was sitting on my nightstand waiting for me.

Did you see Dergal at the weredeer party?

No, I didn't. But I wasn't there long. I just popped in after the boat ride with Jeannie to say hello.

I related what my uncle said to Fiona. "So, considering that, either Dergal is telling the truth, or he left the party to poison my uncle." My stomach rumbled loudly, and Fiona's eyes grew wide. "Sorry. I can't help it. I am so incredibly hungry."

"Why don't you call your Mum and Dad to send you some food and drink?"

"I can't make them fly here just to bring me a sandwich. With a plane ticket, that would be one seriously expensive lunch."

"Use the cauldron," Fiona said as she walked back toward Uncle Phil's tent.

"What cauldron?"

"Ay, Charlotte, what *would* you do without me?" Fiona said with exasperation as she walked back grabbed my arm, and dragged me back toward my uncle's tent.

The yurts that everyone lived in at the circus were circles that divided into four quarter sections (like a pie with massive pieces). My uncle's yurt had one residential pie slice, and three other slices that no one lived in. Each pie slice had its own entry point, and Fiona brought me into the one right next to Uncle Phil's residential slice.

Man, I wanted some pie.

A big juicy apple one, with cinnamon and sugar on top and vanilla bean ice cream melting all over it. My stomach growled again, and I licked my lips imagining the pie, hoping that I could fool my stomach into thinking I had just eaten one.

It didn't work.

"This is the cauldron," Fiona said as she walked me back to a large black iron kettle bubbling rainbow-colored sparkles. It was so big that the rim of it came up to my hip, and the steaming bubbles popped as it boiled. The steam filled the tent with the scent of irises. "You can use it to call anyone paranormal you like, and you'll sort of video chat them. You can also transfer things through it."

"Does the cauldron solve the Wonkavision problem of miniaturization?"

"What is Wonkavision?" Fiona appeared confused.

"Never mind. It's a human movie. It doesn't really exist, it's just a story. Anyway, how do I make this thing work?"

"Just think about a paranormal you wish to communicate with, and the cauldron will find them. As the steam thickens, they'll appear in it. You can't touch them, and they can't touch you, but you *can* pass items back and forth. Like a sandwich."

"Or an apple pie," I drooled.

I stepped up to the cauldron and stared down into the boiling liquid and thought *Mom*. The steam curled taller and taller until it had every appearance of a geyser. There was a bright shimmer, and then my mother appeared smiling within the mist.

"Charlotte? Oh, Charlotte, it's so good to see you! We hoped you would call!"

"I didn't even know about this cauldron until Fiona told me a minute ago, Mom. Sorry, it took me a little bit of time, but I'm still learning my way around here. How come we never talked to Uncle Phil this way?"

"Because your uncle would've had to call us since we don't have a cauldron and…well, you know how he and your father were. Is everything going well? Are you getting settled in?"

"Well, I have a little bit of a problem that I'm hoping you could help me with."

"Sure! What's the problem?"

"Well, we figured out that Uncle Phil was actually poisoned, but we don't know who did it. Since we don't know who did it, we're not sure if they tried to kill Uncle Phil because they were mad at him or because he was the ringmaster. Since someone may have tried to kill the ringmaster, Fiona, Samson, and Uncle Phil are a little worried that I might be poisoned, too. So I haven't eaten. Can you send a sandwich? And maybe some pie?"

My mother's jaw dropped, and she turned away to relate what I had just said to my father. I could vaguely hear her animated side of the conversation, but I couldn't listen to what he was saying.

"Your father wants to know if he should come back. Though honestly, since your father *knew* your Uncle Phil was murdered, I can't understand why he *even came home*. He and I will deal with that, as well as why he didn't tell me," Mom told me rapidly.

Uh-oh.

"No, I don't think so," I told her reluctantly. "I can always call if I think I need him, but honestly Fiona has been stuck to me like glue, and Samson and Uncle Phil both seem to live in my head. Adding one more person to this mix doesn't really seem necessary."

My mother nodded quickly and then turned to relate what I said again to my father. When she wasn't facing whatever she was seeing on her side, her voice became faint as if I heard it through a long tunnel. I could watch her hands animating her discussion with my father, as they no doubt discussed whether he should disregard what I said and come, anyway.

"Um, Mom? Mom. Mom!"

My mother threw up her hand to silence me as her muffled exclamations toward my father became louder. After a good sixty seconds of what I imagined was Dad getting the what for, she turned. "Yes, honey?"

"Bottle of water? Please?"

"Oh my goodness, Charlie, I am so sorry. Just a second." It's too bad Mom couldn't use her *calm-the-heck-down* on herself.

She stepped out of the line of sight of the cauldron's other end while I stared into the mist waiting. "Does the cauldron not follow her?"

"No. Wherever it manifests to connect with the person, it kinda plants itself right there so they can step out of both hearing and view. I think it's so you can't spy on somebody."

"Won't someone notice a shimmery apparition in front of them?"

"It shimmery to *you*. To the paranormals on the other side, it just looks like you're standing there not moving much. There is this whole weird mechanism to 'protect our secrets' and all that hogwash. It protects our secrets all right, but these manifestations make us look *insane*."

"What do you mean?"

"Well, you can't *hear* anybody else on the other side, right? What happens if they talk to you? You won't answer it. You'll just ignore them. Whoever designed this didn't think this through very well," Fiona pointed out. Just then the top of a water bottle poked through the mist. I stared at it. "Just grab it, Charlotte. It won't bite."

I reached forward like Charlie grabbing the Wonka Bar in *Willy Wonka and the Chocolate Factory* and slowly slid the water bottle out of the mist. Unscrewing the top, I gulped half the bottle without taking a breath. "Oh my gosh, it's ice cold. And not poisoned. This is so good. I love this thing."

The edge of a plate poked through, and I grabbed it. A fully dressed overstuffed turkey sandwich, potato chips, and a pile of sweet gherkin pickles covered my mother's everyday china. I placed it on the table next to me and watched the mist hopefully. When an apple poked through, I tried not to be disappointed.

"Thanks, Mom," I said as I placed the apple next to the turkey sandwich.

"Not a problem, Charlie," she said as her image appeared again. "That's my good china though, so make sure to give me that plate back at dinner. If you call around six thirty tonight, I'll make you a plate."

"With apple pie?"

"Not on the dinner plate," she told me. I slapped Fiona's hand as she reached to steal a sweet gherkin pickle and gave her a dirty look. "Do you want me to send over a case of water so that you'll have some? I can run to the store this afternoon."

"No, until we're sure somebody isn't trying to kill me, too, I'd rather not have anything I'm going to eat or drink laying around for too long." My mother's image disappeared and a metal tumbler poked through. I grabbed it and pulled it on to the Midway. "What's this?"

"That tumbler will change color if anything other than water is put into it. If the water isn't pure, the silver metal will turn black. That should at least keep you hydrated while you figure this out."

"Is it magic?"

"No, it's a camping tumbler that I bought at Costco with an advanced water purification sensor. Pretty fancy, huh? Go eat your sandwich, Charlie. Your father and I will run to the store and get you that pie. It seems the least we can do."

"I really appreciate this, Mom. We'll figure it out soon."

"I hope so, Charlie. You were always good at puzzles as a girl, so if anyone can figure it out, I'm sure you can."

"Okay, Mom, I'm going to go. Talk to you tonight."

As the thick steam shimmered away, I turned my full attention to the turkey sandwich. I glared at Fiona as I noticed half of the gherkin pickles were gone.

"What? I haven't eaten, either!" she exclaimed with a mouth full of the stolen pickle.

I felt so much better after having a full meal. I placed my mother's plate next to the cauldron and went back to my uncle's residential yurt slice.

I still really wanted pie.

Once inside, Fiona and I sat on my uncle's bed next to Samson to talk about our next move. "This is such a man cave," Fiona observed as she ran her eyes over the interior.

"Well, Uncle Phil was a bachelor. It *is* his yurt."

Actually, since you are the ringmaster now this is actually your yurt. The location is picked so that I can get to the back of the lot or the front or the middle without much walking, Uncle Phil told me.

"Walking is good for you, Uncle Phil."

I doubt it would've made me immune to poison, so clearly I made the right decision not to exercise and to provide for my own comfort in life, Uncle Phil pointed out as he peeked through the screen. *In any case, you can decorate this place any way you wish. It's yours now, dear girl.*

"I don't really have time to decorate, Uncle Phil."

"Super crazy cosmic power, Charlotte," Fiona singsonged. "You can blink and change this whole place from top to bottom."

"Let's just hold off on that for now. I don't want to blink some important piece of evidence out of existence just to make the room look airier. Like the herbs. Is there any way we can figure out what the poison was? Like with my superpowers?"

You can do many things, Samson said. *But you cannot know many things. Your power manifests action. You cannot manifest knowledge. Knowing must be learned or earned.*

"That makes sense, though it's a little disappointing," I grumbled. "Do we have, like, some paranormal FBI with a Crime Scene Investigation unit?"

Of course, Uncle Phil said. *The Witches' Council. They have a Forensic Magic Department. Same thing.*

"Well, shoot. That's not going to work." Fiona held up her hands to remind me she had absolutely no clue what the heck I was talking about since she could only hear one side of the conversation.

"The Witches' Council. We'd have to ask them for help. They have a Forensic Magic Department."

"Right, but you don't have to open up a case," she pointed out. "You're essentially a mayor, and a sheriff all rolled into one, so you're part of the government. Technically, anyway. You can just contact the nerds and pass a plant through the cauldron to the lab, and they'll test it for you."

Fiona is correct, dear girl, Uncle Phil agreed. *We don't need to open a case or ask them to investigate.*

I went over to the dead black plants. Their dirt contained shards of the glass that had shattered, and the pottery that the plants had grown in was burned. It appeared the pottery had been scorched by fire, or chemically burned by acid.

"I don't want to touch it," I murmured. "It

actually did damage to the pots. If it did damage to the pots, what kind of damage is it going to do my skin if I handle it?" Fiona paused as we stared at the damaged pots.

"Well, if you don't want to touch it, we're going to have to call the Witches' Council police. They would be the ones to collect evidence."

"But if the Witches' Council is responsible, they're going to know we're looking into it."

Just pick the pot up. It can't hurt you unless you eat it, Samson said.

"No! I don't want my skin to melt off," I told the cat.

"What is he saying?" Fiona asked. My frustration at playing a near-constant game of telephone between the ghost, the cat, and my friend exploded.

"I wish you could hear that damn cat! This is such a pain!"

Well, she can't, so learn to handle it, Samson answered haughtily.

"Ay, actually I can," Fiona said in surprise as her eyes grew wide. She gaped at Samson. "I heard what you said clear as a bell."

You can't. You're not even a witch, Samson warned as he stood up and his hair rose on his back.

"I can, ya cheeky bugger. I even heard your snotty tone of voice," Fiona countered as she walked over to the little black cat. Samson's eyes narrowed as he grew more agitated.

Now see what you did? I told you to get a hold of yourself, Samson spat angrily. *Now you made it so horse-face can hear what I think. In all my years of being the Astley familiar I don't think I've ever been so insulted in my life.*

"Hey now!" Fiona shouted. "No need to be insulted or insulting, ya ken?"

"Samson, you told me that you are here to prevent me from making mistakes so if I just made one, it's pretty much your fault, isn't it? Because I sure as heck don't know what I'm doing, and you haven't been all that much help, either. While I've been traipsing around this fairground trying not to get killed, you were napping. You don't like it? Pay more attention."

Red electricity snapped around the cat as he stared at me like I was a mouse he caught in a corner. A tiny voice in the back of my head warned me I was going too far, but Uncle Phil remained silent, and so I pushed the cat further. "You don't like it? Undo it."

I can't, Samson growled. I could feel waves of hostility coming from him.

"Why not? I thought you could do anything I could do and more?"

Samson sat up on the bed and his eyes flashed in my direction. The cat's ears were forward, and his tail swished back and forth in jerky, angry motions.

I cannot undo what the ringmaster has done. I can prevent a mistake, I can help you undo a mistake, but you are the ringmaster. What you want to be done may not be destroyed by your familiar. What you want to be done may not be stopped by your familiar if it causes no harm. The power is yours, and the choices are yours. Now undo what you have done!

Despite Samson's anger, I felt like I had won a power struggle with the little cat, and Samson knew it. It was a power struggle I had barely become aware of before I won it, and part of me was ecstatic. Take that, you stubborn cat.

"No. I also wish that Fiona could hear Uncle Phil."

Can you hear me, Fiona? Uncle Phil asked hopefully.

"Ya, I can hear you," she said as she looked around for the origin of the disembodied voice now echoing in her head. "I can't see you, though. It's good to hear your voice again, old friend." Fiona's eyes filled with tears.

Now, none of that. This will certainly be easier, at least while I'm here. Uncle Phil seemed as if he wanted to say something else, and then he stopped. Glancing with concern at the cat sitting stiffly on the bed, he swallowed. *Samson will no doubt get over it.*

Don't count on it, Samson hissed resentfully.

CHAPTER 7

So.

Samson was *furious*.

An hour later, the cat still glowed with a thick red aura as he sat alert on the bed, forcefully telegraphing his fury into my brain. It hadn't been my intent to infuriate the cat to this extent...Ugh. Even when I think I'm winning, I somehow wind up mucking things up.

I had usually done well with learning by doing. Often that was my *preferred* way to learn new skills, really.

There was a nagging suspicion in the back of my mind as I stared at the volcano-colored feline, though, that learning to be something close to an omnipotent being by blundering into magic I hadn't thought through was perhaps not the best way to become an excellent ringmaster.

I thought I was taking charge. I was even proud of myself for just making sure Fiona could hear Samson and Uncle Phil without waiting for anyone to approve. I sent the Witches' Council back, I made communication easier.

Go me, right?

Now, though, I felt queasy watching my new familiar stew in a deadly quiet cat rage on the bed as his eyes followed me aggressively. He appeared to be plotting something if the thwacks of his tail were any indication. For sure.

I needed to set aside the hunt for the murderer and find out a bit more from Uncle Phil. From the looks of it, I was in mortal danger from Samson right now while the hypothetical murderer was just a maybe.

"Uncle Phil, now that we've got the food and drink situation worked out, for now, can you maybe sit down with me for a little bit and explain some of this stuff? Can Samson, like, punish me because he's angry at me? I feel like I should know things like this before I put my foot in it." I glanced at Samson nervously. "Again."

Uncle Phil nodded and sat down in a chair next to the bed.

That's a good idea, dear girl, he told me. *We certainly wouldn't want you to put your foot in a magical pile of poo, now would we?*

Uncle Phil turned to Fiona and asked if she would mind giving us some privacy for a while. My friend smiled at me and left the tent, letting me know she'd be back in a couple of hours.

Now, do you have any specific questions before I get started?

"Is there anything I *can't* do?"

Well, of course, there is, Uncle Phil laughed. *Bullet-pointing those things will fly in one ear and right out the other. Let's go back to the beginning, hundreds of years ago when the first ringmaster crafted the magic to protect this place.*

The air shimmered between us, and with a ghostly glow, a square appeared on the floor with many ghostly figures walking upon it. They were the size of small toys, a miniaturized version of a scene that took place in a time long past.

These are our ancestors, Uncle Phil explained. *This is a re-creation of the moment that the Magical Midway power coalesced within my great-grandmother many times removed.*

"How many generations does this go back?"

Twelve generations back. You are the thirteenth generation of Astleys to bear the title ringmaster.

"Ugh. Really? That seems ominous. Isn't thirteen bad luck?"

Not in our world, dear girl. In our world, thirteen is a number of immense power and significance. My uncle gestured downward and my gaze returned to the tiny ghostly figures on the little ghostly field as they gathered themselves into a circle and raised their arms.

With a bright flash, fog and lightning bolts surrounded one figure in the center of the circle. After what seemed like several minutes, the chaotic storm around her dissipated and she fell to her hands and knees to the ground. *And so it is done. That was the moment that the Astleys agreed to host the magic of the Midway.*

"Host the magic? So we didn't create it?"

No, we joined with it.

"Oh, I see."

I didn't.

Each successive generation created rules and limitations within the magic, he continued, as the scene within the shimmering square changed. A new group of people, and a new tiny figure in the center. The scene flipped one after another after another, as I watched each ancestor that came before me accept, and receive, and become infused by the Magical Midway power. Some were women, some were men, some were older, and some were younger. All were Astleys, and I was a direct descendant of the bloodline history I watched flip like a sparkler-infused PowerPoint.

And we end with your own elevation to ringmaster. I watched as my own little ghostly figure was surrounded by fog and lightning. She collapsed to the ground, and I winced.

Each person you've seen here shaped, and changed, and limited, and stretched the bounds of the power. They also limited, and condensed, and drew its boundaries. Much like a story that is added to and changed by each successive author that retells it, so, too, has the power been added to and changed by each one of us.

"And no one kept, like, a rulebook or overview of what can be done and what can't be done?"

All of us are not beholden to those who have gone before. If someone who has gone before made a rule, the newest ringmaster would have the power to change that rule, Uncle Phil explained. *Except when they find they don't.*

"Well, that's as clear as mud," I mumbled.

The power of the Magical Midway that now infuses you is not a thing, Charlotte. It is not inanimate energy without consciousness. As I've told you before, we do not know how the circuses came to be or how such power was invested in single-family bloodlines. We do know that the Midway's power seems to have a will. It has a focus, perhaps even an agenda. It will allow you to act as its agent for the protection of those here and the service of those humans that visit here. But we have never truly understood what its ultimate goal is.

"Wait a minute," I stammered. "Are you telling me that I'm basically being possessed by some omnipotent spirit or whatever that lends me its power?"

That would be a fairly accurate assessment, Charlotte.

This would've been great information to have before I agreed to allow some omnipotent superpower hitch a ride on my person for this lifetime. For the first time since I had decided to do this, I was a little afraid.

This power has never been anything other than benevolent to us and all those that come here, Uncle Phil pointed out as he watched my face grow anxious. *In thirteen generations, no harm has ever befallen an Astley because of this power.*

"But if what you're saying is true, this power or being, or whatever probably knew that your food was poisoned. I mean, if it's omnipotent.

And it let you die! That seems like harm to me, Uncle Phil."

Perhaps it was my time, Charlotte, my uncle pointed out gently. *Perhaps it was your time to take over. Life itself for paranormals and humans moves in mysterious ways. We share control with the universe, dear girl. There is free will within our fate. But never doubt we each have a fate. What matters is the choices we make as we face that fate.*

"Okay, let's get a little less college philosophy class for a sec," I said. "Why are there no other witches at the Midway?"

The energy that animates this place is... uncomfortable for them if they are not of our particular nature. Uncle Phil leaned forward and placed his elbows on his knees. *We make them very insecure, and for powerful beings that is not a feeling they willingly wish to feel. The power that we hold is so far beyond what they are able to access that they give us a wide berth. Since you are new, you are at the weakest you will ever be in knowledge and skill, and so the Council came to test you.*

"What about the other circus?"

The Makepeace Circus? What about them?

"Do they have the same super spirit kind of thing that we do or are they something different?"

Uncle Phil sat back and smiled. *They have a super spirit, as you call it, too. It is not the same as ours, I don't think. What I mean is, it's the same type of spirit but not the same consciousness. At least I have never had any indication of a link.*

"So they are different people, basically?" Uncle Phil winced at my trivializing phrasing but nodded. "Do they like each other? I mean, do we ever take the circuses and put them next to each other so the two super spirits can talk or something?" He shook his head no.

We've never been pulled to do that. I assume they can communicate with one another some other way, or they have no desire to.

This was a lot to take in.

For a witch raised by lapsed witches in the human world, this all seemed like information I should have had *years ago,* so I could adjust to it without the pressure of being *responsible* for it.

I could do nothing about it now, so I just tried to take a deep breath and think through my new reality.

"Have *you* ever tried to talk to it? This super spirit?"

Of course, Uncle Phil said with surprise. *Every day I was the ringmaster."* He glanced over at the glowing-red cat still sitting angrily on the bed.

My stomach dropped to my ankles. Samson quietly but menacingly continued to stare with narrowed eyes. His tail whipped back and forth in his silence.

"Oh, come on. No way."

Well, he is not the actual super spirit, but he is your conduit to it.

"So the super spirit is ticked off at me because he is?"

No, but the super spirit's conduit is ticked off at you, and that could pose a problem for you in the future.

Samson hissed, and I buried my head in my hands.

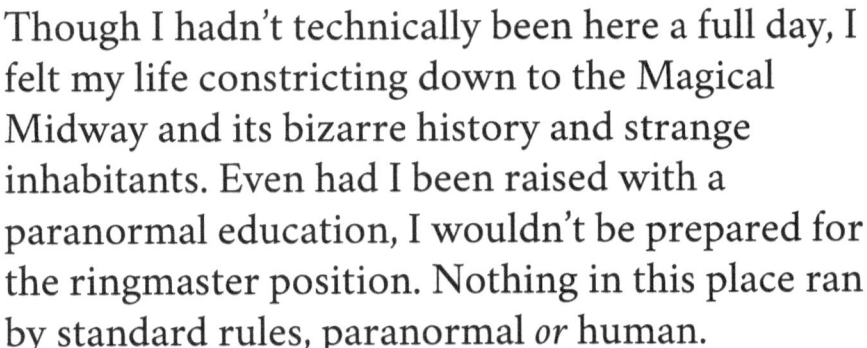

Though I hadn't technically been here a full day, I felt my life constricting down to the Magical Midway and its bizarre history and strange inhabitants. Even had I been raised with a paranormal education, I wouldn't be prepared for the ringmaster position. Nothing in this place ran by standard rules, paranormal *or* human.

I needed some air.

As I walked along the path toward the Big Top, people I vaguely knew smiled at me. Many tilted their head in acknowledgment and went on about their way. The Magical Midway had not been opened to human visitors since Uncle Phil's death, and the usually frantic energy of work and preparation was much more subdued.

As I turned the corner out of Yurt Row, I caught the smarmy centaur Dergal sandwiched between two screaming women twenty feet in front of me. On his right, Stephanie Clodion poked her finger into his chiseled chest as she released her fury upon him. On his left, Alessandra Atwater wept tears of anger.

I had to give the guy credit. I wouldn't want to stand between a furious naiad and an angry satyress.

"You promised me that you would be faithful! You swore it would never happen again!" Alessandra wailed as her fist thumped against Dergal's thick, muscled arm. "Yet here you still stand, and you humiliate me with the goat-woman as your latest indignity flung in my direction!"

"And you are no satyr, Dergal! I do not allow those that I pair with to enjoy the fun that we satyrs are *entitled* to. I will not share one of my groupings with some weepy, jealous naiad!"

"Ladies, ladies, come on now," Dergal purred

as he stood strong and unmoved by their blows or their anger. "I love you both in my own way. There's no need for all this *drama*."

"*Drama*," Alessandra spat contemptuously as she whacked him again, and fury flashed across Dergal's face. As her arm blazed toward his shoulder, I spotted a nasty bruise on her forearm. "You should not be breathing the air of this Midway to participate in any kind of drama, you disloyal, disreputable, manipulative *lout*. You think too much of yourself!"

I stepped back behind the carousel and watched the scene play out. Other paranormals quietly walked by, ignoring the threesome screaming next to the weredeer pen. A few eyes peeked quickly at the love triangle, shook their heads, and walked faster to get away from the group.

I wasn't sure what to do.

Was I in charge of coming between these people and managing their embarrassing fallouts? Did I just let personal issues like this work themselves out? I didn't know.

I reached out to each participant to read them. Stephanie was angry, but not so mad that I would call it rage or think her out of control. Dergal was smug and amused at the two women's emotional state. Alessandra was…frightened. And very sad.

"I wish that poison had killed *you*! You are a liar!" Alessandra Atwater screamed as she turned on her heel and stomped back toward the Charybdis Boat Ride.

"Put yourself out to pasture, horse-man," Stephanie told him as she, too, turned on her heel away from him and headed toward the *Milk Bottle* game. "You are not smart enough to win the games you're playing!" she called over her shoulder.

"Wow," I said out loud to myself.

"Wow, indeed," an unfamiliar voice answered. I whipped my head around and spotted one of the newer members of the Midway, Fortuna Delphi.

The petite woman was the picture of a fortune teller with ruby red lips, dark hair, and flowing layers of peasant clothing. Fluttering silk scarves dripped from her hair and limbs, and bells tinkled in the wind.

"When I came out of my tent I saw you and thought I would come over to say hello. That was quite a scene, was it not?"

"I hope that doesn't happen when the humans

are here," I told Fortuna. I stuck out my hand and introduced myself formally.

"Never present your hand to a fortune teller unless you wish it to be read," Fortuna laughed as she waved it away and curtsied in response. "It is nice to meet you, Ms. Astley. I wasn't here long enough to know your uncle well, but he gave me a place when I feared I would find none. I was very grateful for that."

"You came from the Langdon Circus, didn't you?"

"I did," she nodded, and her expression grew wistful and sad. "It was my home for fourteen years. Ever since my visit as a teenager to the Langdon Circus woke up my latent ability."

Fortuna motioned for me to follow her into her tent, and I did so. Once inside, my nose filled with the scent of blue roses while my eyes adjusted to the gentle smoky dimness of the woman's reading room. "Tea?"

My mouth felt drier at the suggestion though I politely declined. Refusing food and drink from everyone that I met or reconnected with at Magical Midway would be a real pain in the keister. Plus the fact that it felt rude. "Someone told me you were actually human. I didn't think there were any humans in paranormal towns or fairs."

"Somewhere in my ancestry, there is no doubt a witch or elf or some creature with the gift of intuition and foresight. As it was explained to me, stepping into the barrier of a paranormal fair can awaken that latent ability in some humans. Even when it's been dormant for generations."

I didn't know that. The stuff that I didn't know seemed to pile up into a tower of information. In all these generations, no one wrote all this down? Really?

"Since humans cannot enter the paranormal towns," Fortuna continued. "Someone with the ability would have to come to a fair for it to happen, so it happening at all is exceedingly rare. Further, they would have to recognize what's happening before they leave again and it returns to dormancy."

"So you're kind of a unicorn."

"No, I cannot shapeshift," Fortuna responded.

"No, I mean…ah, never mind. So if you leave the fair, you lose the ability?"

"Yes," Fortuna nodded as she motioned toward a chair. "When off these grounds, I am a regular human with no more or less insight than a regular human would have. You see now why I was very grateful to your uncle for allowing me a place here."

"That's…that's both beautiful and tragic."

"I agree," Fortuna smiled as she pushed a wayward curl from her eyes. "Your choice to permit me a place here allows me to keep being the seer that I believe I was meant to be. I thought it important you knew that in case you were unaware."

"If Uncle Phil brought you on, I can't see any reason why I would change anything. Honestly, I don't know enough *to* change anything yet, really."

"But you could. I would prefer not to find myself one day sitting in a field alone as my world disappears without me."

I tilted my head and raised my eyebrow, confused.

"The ringmaster must agree that someone can stay. You must decide the petitioner can be a part of the community, and once you decide in favor of us, we are tied to it. While other paranormals can enter the grounds, they will *remain* on the physical land when you move the Magical Midway to its next location unless you accept them as residents. Only then does the magic of the Midway include them, too."

"Wow, that's harsh. But good to know. Sometimes I feel like everyone knows more about this whole thing than I do," I told Fortuna with some self-pitying frustration.

"We each know the parts well that are relevant to us," she told me, and then sipped her tea daintily. "Not all parts are relevant, and not all parts are known. The two midways that remain are the two last truly mysterious magics left in the world. Their secrets have yet to be fully understood," Fortuna said, and then paused dramatically. "Perhaps they are not meant to be."

I left Fortuna's tent feeling like I might have made another friend. In all my years visiting, I had made some acquaintances at the Magical Midway. Fiona was the only paranormal I would call a true friend.

With only a week, I just never put myself out there. Admittedly, there were other reasons, too.

Some, like the Larry brothers, were hard to picture as real friends. Every brother other than Bob appeared unable to speak more than one word in a sentence most of the time. Even had I met them previously, I couldn't see myself hanging out for the evening with Kat and Ari Riddle. Hours of the sphinxes rhyming in casual conversation would likely give me a migraine headache.

Fortuna Delphi, however, seemed like someone I could hang with.

Before I left her tent, she suggested that I check on Alessandra Atwater, the sad naiad from the earlier love triangle confrontation.

Alessandra had been getting readings and counseling from Fortuna for several weeks. Like a priest holding a penitent's confession sacrosanct, the fortune teller refused to share with me the reason for her suggestion, but was insistent that she be my next stop.

I walked past the mentalist's tent. Stepping behind the Haunted House, I came upon the naiads' beautiful boat ride. The log flume twisted, rose, fell, and doubled over on itself in the relatively small space. The human riders got much more than their money's worth, as well as a unique experience that could not have been duplicated in a non-magical amusement park.

"Ringmaster!" Anya, one of the naiad sisters, called as she stepped out from behind a waterfall. "Congratulations on your elevation! It's about damn time we got a woman running this show."

The naiad's red hair was cropped short and spiky. Feminist slogan patches covered her blue jean jacket. Military-colored cargo pants and black steel-toed tactical boots completed the ensemble. Anya looked like she was prepared for a women's march to break out at any moment.

"Thank you, though I wish that happened in a much different way," I told her firmly shaking her extended hand. Ow. As she mercifully released me, I flexed my fingers to make sure none of the bones were broken. "I was actually stopping by to check on Alessandra. I saw an argument between her, Dergal, and Stephanie."

"Mud puddles! Those sisters of mine, still so stuck in the whole bring a man under your spell, make him love you, decide whether or not to drown him in the lake thing."

"You drown men in lakes?"

"Well, not recently."

"Oh. Well, that's a good thing. I think."

"I suppose that depends on the man and whether he needs drowning," Anya laughed. "No worries, ringmaster, one of the things we oathed to when we joined the Magical Midway is that we would cause no harm. That includes drowning people even if they need killing."

"Is there some magical limitation on you?

Like, if you kill someone, you'll suddenly find yourself outside the boundary unable to get back in?"

"Nope. But how likely is it that you won't figure out it's one of us if some Lothario is suddenly floating face down in our log flume?"

I shrugged. "Good point."

"And that's why we don't drown them," Anya said as she held her hands wide.

"So what *do* you do?"

Anya turned away and motioned for me to follow her through the waterfall. "My sister Alessandra is here in the operations room for the boat ride. I'll take you to her if you follow me."

Well, that was a question avoidance if I ever saw one. It wasn't even a deft avoidance. I didn't have much of a paranormal education, but I studied mythology in high school. If some of the myths that surrounded these nymphs were correct, I had to wonder why any man would date the Atwaters.

Anya disappeared right through the cascading waterfall of water.

Stretching my hand forward I placed my fingertips under the water nervously and was shocked to find I felt no wetness. What the heck is this? I thrust my hand through and felt energy tingle.

As I passed under the streams, I felt cleansed in a way I rarely had before. My tense muscles were relaxed, my hair fluffy, and my numerous concerns felt lighter. As I emerged out the other side of the enclosed operations area, I gasped.

"Damn cool, isn't it?" Anya laughed. "I love seeing people's faces after they go under it for the first time."

"What *is* it? It's amazing."

"We don't have magic the way you witches have magic, but we can make water do almost anything that we want it to. We can have it curse or cleanse or make folks happy or make them sad. That particular waterfall is like a three-second spa day," Anya explained. "It gives you the results of a spa day without having to waste ten hours sitting in the steam room, getting a massage, getting a facial, and having your chakras and energy aligned."

"Well, I definitely feel aligned," I told her.

"The effects only last for a couple of hours, unfortunately," Alessandra said in a hoarse whisper from the corner of a small alcove off the larger room. "Lately, I feel I should just put my chair under there and stay. Good afternoon, ringmaster."

"Could everyone please just call me Charlotte? This whole ringmaster title thing just makes me feel weird."

"Of course, Ringmaster Charlotte," Anya said.

"No, just Charlotte. No ringmaster. I'm just Charlotte."

"You are definitely not *just* anything. Only two women before you have been ringmasters of the Magical Midway even though the founding Astley was a woman! You should be proud to wield the title. I bet the centaurs are having bloody apoplexy at the thought!" Anya laughed uproariously as Alessandra's chin dropped to her chest with closed eyes.

"Are you okay, Alessandra? I don't mean to pry, but I saw the brouhaha with Dergal and Stephanie on the Midway. I wanted to come to check on you, make sure you are okay."

"Thank you for your concern, Charlotte," the delicate blonde nymph whispered. "I do not know why I let myself feel such pain over his treatment of me. I should have learned by now that he is not to be trusted. Yet, I keep going back."

"I told you he was bad news," Anya told her.

The tough-looking woman went over to her sister and leaned down beside her. "You deserve better than that horrible centaur." Alessandra nodded and pulled her long sleeves down over her wrists clutching them in her fists like a child.

"I also wanted to ask you about that bruise on your arm. It looked kind of nasty." Alessandra paled at my question as Anya stared back at me with confusion. The quiet woman clutched the sleeves in her hands tighter, crossing her arms.

"Show me," Anya said sharply. She turned back toward her sister and reached out toward Alessandra's wrist. Alessandra shook her head no, vigorously pulling away from her sister and pressing her body against the wall. "I mean it, Alessandra. Show me your arms."

Tears poured down the naiad's face as she slumped in response to her sister's demands. Alessandra unclenched her fists and opened her palms. Anya pulled up the two sleeves of the sweater and gasped as she saw the black and purple bruises up and down her sister's arms. As I stepped closer, I could see the outline of thick fingers.

"I don't even have to ask who did this to you. Oh, sister, why did you hide this? How could you go back to that horrible excuse for a man?" The tough as nails Anya teared up as she caressed the hair of her wounded sister. "You will stay away from him from now on, do you hear me?"

"I will," Alessandra said. "I had made him angry. He found me at the weredeer party without him, and he had told me not to go. I know how jealous he can be, so I should've known better. It wasn't entirely his fault."

"The hell it wasn't," I told the two nymphs angrily. They startled and glanced up at me as if they had forgotten I was there. "Dergal did this, I assume?"

"Yes, but he didn't realize how tightly he was squeezing me. The magician, the new one from the Langdon Circus, came out as we were passing by the front of his tent. I suppose he overheard us and he interceded."

"What happened then?" I asked Alessandra.

"He made Dergal let go, and then walked me back to the waterfall. Men cannot pass beyond its waters, so Mark made sure I got safely beyond its mists. I don't know where he went after that."

I glanced back toward the waterfall, but I could see nothing outside.

I didn't know much about Mark Botsworth, but I knew he was a human that had telekinetic abilities that must have awakened like Fortuna

Delphi's when he came to the Langdon Circus.
He performed mentalist feats for the humans, but
he had no other power I was aware of.

Interceding against an aggressive centaur to
protect Alessandra was an impressively brave act.
Centaurs were notoriously strong—as
Alessandra's arms could, unfortunately, attest to.

"I want you to stay away from Dergal," I told
her, surprised at my own vehemence. "No one
should put hands on anyone else at the Magical
Midway, and no one should have reason to be
afraid of anyone else."

"You'll let me drown him?" Anya asked me
hopefully.

"I have to admit the thought has crossed my
mind since I saw her arms," I told her. "But no, I
don't think drowning Dergal is the way we need
to go here. As satisfying as that might be for
everyone in this room."

"I told you, ringmaster, some people need
killing," Anya pointed out.

"Who has a right to decide that?"

"Well. You. You are the ringmaster," Anya told
me as if my powers of life and death over all the
residents of the Magical Midway were obvious.
"We all agreed to be subject to your judgment."

"In the human world, battering your partner

would get you jail time. There will definitely be some sort of consequences for Dergal. First, though, I need to fully understand everything he's done." Anya nodded as Alessandra covered her face with her hands.

"I will make sure until then that he can't hurt anybody else," I promised them both. "At least, I will as soon as someone tells me how I do that."

"Ask the cat," Anya said.

"Right. The cat."

I suggested that Anya and Alessandro stay within the protection of the waterfall until I gave them the all clear, and left the boat ride to go patch up the relationship with my familiar.

CHAPTER 8

"Samson, are you in here?" I called as I
entered Uncle Phil's yurt.

Silence greeted me. Oppressive, angry,
judgmental silence.

My eyes scanned the interior, looking for the
origin of the negative emotions I could feel
hitting me in waves. Closer to the sleeping area, I
spotted the red-black glow of anger still curled
up on the coverlet. The cat's sensitive funnel ears
moved as I did, indicating awareness of my
presence despite Samson's total lack of
acknowledgment.

"Are you ignoring me now?"

Silence. Ears flicked.

"Look," I said as I climbed up to the middle of

the king-sized bed and sat cross-legged before him. "I will fully admit that I don't know what I'm doing. I'm trying, but this is completely different from anything I experienced in the human world. There are rules and differences and unwritten requirements that I don't know yet. If I violated one and it hurt your feelings, I am truly sorry."

The cat raised its head and yawned. With a serpentine grace, he lifted his body to step away from me, walked two feet up the bed, and lowered his body back down into a sphinx-like position.

Well, at least he was awake and looking at me.

"Samson, I don't really know what else to say. I don't really understand what I did that made you so angry, so I don't know how to apologize for it or make it any better."

Our bond is unlike any other bond between two creatures in the world, Samson sent imperiously. *Opening up our bond to others is just not done. You desecrated our relationship.*

"I didn't mean to. I didn't know, Samson," I told him as I reached out to pet his head. Samson hissed as my fingers neared his nose and I pulled back. Oh, boy.

I wracked my brain for everything I knew and everything I understood about the cats back at the shelter to find some way to communicate to this omnipotent cat that I valued him.

I stared into his eyes and slowly blinked.

Stop that, Samson snapped. *You look ridiculous.*

I slow-blinked again and sighed a deep sigh.

You know how to do that, but you were ignorant of the offense of opening my voice to your horse friend? Truly? Samson asked with more imperiousness tinged with incredulity.

"I truly didn't realize Samson. With Uncle Phil having been murdered, I really just felt it was easier for all of us to talk since we're all trying to unravel what happened. It just kept me from playing go-between. I'm really, really sorry if I didn't understand what it meant."

You should not have to understand. Just know. Just feel. It just is, Samson told me as he stood up.

"I'm not singularly intuitive, Samson."

Your very power is intuition! Before you were even the ringmaster! Samson spat as his fur puffed out from his body.

"Okay, I'm not *magically* intuitive. I can sense that you're angry. Very angry with me. But that's a simple emotion. I can't sense a tie between us. That's not a talent that I have."

If a cat could roll its eyes, I would swear Samson rolled his eyes at me. He stood up with a flourish and walked across the bed to climb into my lap. As he settled in, one paw came to rest on my thigh. Samson extended his claws gently and dug his needle-like nails ever so slightly through the denim and into my flesh.

See who we are, he thought.

A vortex exploded within my mind. I threw my arms back and clutched the bed to steady myself from the dizzying onslaught. Images flashed one after the other like a rapid-fire slide-show.

Samson and I were wrapped in a cocoon of twinkling pink and blue and white light, tendrils of silvery pink cords that spread all over the Midway and connected us to each inhabitant. Some cords stretched beyond the boundary to inhabitants that had left the Midway but were still bound magically to it.

Do you see it? Samson asked. I was so overwhelmed I couldn't answer.

The last picture revealed our bright cocoon with a thick silver cord jutting above us like a trunk to a dome of energy that spread out to encompass the entire Magical Midway. The dome shimmered and flickered and sparkled.

In the center of the dome, the image of the first ringmaster glowed with a blinding iridescence. Then there was another ringmaster and another ringmaster. With each new conjuring of my ancestors, the loyal Samson's image remained unchanging beside each one.

Just beyond Samson's vision, I thought I glimpsed an image in the dome. A smiling face, so bright that I couldn't look at it. Just as I thought I would finally glimpse it entirely, the vortex of energy and sound and light disappeared from my mind as quickly as it had overtaken it.

That is who we are, Samson told me as he lifted his head. *We are linked. We are not we. We are not two. We are now one.*

"I understand," I gasped as I wiped the sweat from my brow (even though I didn't completely understand). Despite not having moved, I felt as if I had just run a marathon. My heart pounded in my chest.

After a few silent minutes of deep breathing, my heart rate returned to a steady state, and I felt able to speak again. "Thank you for showing me that. I am really sorry. I know I need you in this, Samson. I'll undo it. I just thought it would be easier."

It is easier not to protect the bond, Samson told me. *But a weak or breached relationship can put everything that you just saw at risk.*

I nodded and reached down to caress the soft fur of the cat. I felt I understood him a little better than before. Samson was snarky, and judgmental, and haughty, and a butt sometimes.

He was also two hundred years old or more and knew much more about this than I did. He knew what the face in the energy dome was, while I did not understand how to even process what I had seen.

I whispered words to undo what I had done at the cauldron. I sensed the expansion snap like a bungee tendril of energy I snipped with scissors.

Thank you, Samson said, and he laid down his head on my lap. A soft purr emanated from him.

"Anytime," I told him affectionately. "But when you're done with your nap? We have a problem."

It will still be there when I am done. I just need a few moments. Then we will deal with the latest catastrophe, Samson sighed.

When Samson was done re-bonding and cuddling, we did a quick cocoon around Dergal so he could hurt no one else. Samson then directed me to go find Fiona, while he called Uncle Phil back to the yurt.

We gathered yet again in my uncle's living quarters. While Fiona could still hear Uncle Phil, she now could not listen to any of Samson's communication.

"So at this point we know Jeannie said that Dergal took the cup," I told them. "Dergal says he didn't take the cup. Alessandra says that Dergal dragged her out of the weredeer party, Dergal says he was never at the weredeer party. By the way, Dergal is a violent jerk, so he moved to the top of the suspect list."

"He *is* somewhat of a sleazeball, but I am curious as to why you have decided he is violent?" Fiona asked.

"I saw an argument between him and Stephanie, the satyress, and Alessandra, the blonde naiad sister. Apparently, he's dating both of them and lying to each woman that she's the only one. What *really* concerned me, though, are the bruises on Alessandra's arms. She says that he dragged her out of the weredeer party, and Mark Botsworth interceded to get her away from him. I saw the bruises. They are *really* nasty. Bruises like that don't happen by accident."

"Anya is going to cut his b—well, she's going

to be very upset," Fiona pointed out. I nodded in agreement.

"Anya was there when I talked to Alessandra. Let's just say she wasn't pleased."

"I'm not pleased, either. However, I do not have steel-toed combat boots and a seven-inch hunting knife that says #timesup," Fiona said. "Had Dergal physically abused her before?"

I shrugged in response. "I didn't ask. It didn't matter. It was enough the man did it once."

"True."

I am so surprised, Uncle Phil said. *Dergal seemed like such a polite young man. And he's a wonderful mechanic.*

Fiona and I peered sympathetically at each other and tried desperately not to roll our eyes.

What? What did I say?

"Uncle Phil, the fact that he seems polite and is a good mechanic has nothing to do with what we're talking about. He didn't seem friendly to me, by the way. He seemed like a snake."

But he's such a handsome young man, all the girls seem to love him!

"You know, Anya was really excited about having a woman as the ringmaster of the Magical Midway. I'm starting to see why," I told Fiona as I leaned in toward her. She nodded knowingly and

smiled patronizingly in the general direction of
Uncle Phil's disembodied voice.

"Since you're dead now, Uncle Phil, Fiona and
I will not give you a lecture or explain to you why
you are not woke. If you were alive, though, we'd
set aside a couple of hours."

I am awake. I'm not napping. I'm completely
paying attention here! Uncle Phil protested. This
time, I rolled my eyes.

I am woke, Samson interjected. *Cats have had*
matriarchal societal structures for eons.

"Okay, enough. We're getting sidetracked," I
told the assembled group. "Nothing I learned this
afternoon gives me any more insight into why
someone would kill Uncle Phil. But I had a
thought as I was coming back from talking to the
naiads. What if Uncle Phil *wasn't* the target?"

Come again? Uncle Phil asked, surprised.

"According to Jeannie, Dergal had the cup.
Dergal is clearly lying to us about something, and
he's *not* an honest guy. I saw the argument with
Stephanie and Alessandra. I saw her bruises. I've
also seen all this in less than a day. What if he *did*
get the cup from Jeannie—but he wasn't quick
about bringing it to Uncle Phil's tent?"

"You're saying that maybe someone tried to
poison Dergal," Fiona said as she snapped her

fingers. "That's totally believable. I mean, I kind of want to kill him right now myself, and I didn't see *any* of this with my own eyes."

"It doesn't explain why he is lying about being at the weredeer party, or why he's lying about having the drink," I said.

"No, it doesn't," Uncle Phil said.

"Then that's the next thing we need to find out."

Fiona and I left Uncle Phil and walked toward the Big Top. To my surprise, Samson hopped down off the bed and followed closely behind us as we sought the leader of the weredeer. Uncle Phil had explained that the weredeer were one of the more populous groups at the Midway, and Avalon was the alpha doe of the matriarchal group.

"There she is," Fiona said as she pointed to a demure-looking woman seated under a canopy next to the entrance to the Big Top. Her pretty brown hair and pixie-like features were not particularly attention-getting, but her posture immediately drew my eye. Avalon seemed to be poised to bolt, and her eyes flicked around warily in all directions at regular intervals.

"Do all shapeshifters have some aspect of their creature natures in human form? It's like she senses a hunting stand while foraging during deer season. She's practically quivering."

"Simple shapeshifters, yes."

"As opposed to more complex shapeshifters?"

"As opposed to magical creatures that can shapeshift into an animal," Fiona said with some exasperation. "A kelpie isn't a shapeshifter. A kelpie is a kelpie, and we can shapeshift. Surely you know the difference, ya?"

"No."

Fiona stopped walking and stared at me, her mouth gaping.

"Come now, be serious, Charlotte," she said.

"I *am* serious. Honestly, Fiona. I had no idea."

Fiona poked me in the chest as she stepped close, and said accusingly: "All these years we've been friends, you thought I was *simply* some horse shapeshifter?"

"I guess I never really thought about it," I told her as I carefully backed up. She stomped her foot loudly, and I did my best not to laugh at the very horselike expression of her annoyance. Fiona apparently would not be amused at my observation, and I decided my health might depend on my ability to keep some things to myself.

Wise choice, Samson projected.

Thank you, I thought back.

"Charlotte, you don't seem to think about much," Fiona said as she patted me on the head. "You have human air between the ears. Not even paranormal air. Human air. *Uneducated* human air."

"Okay, brainiac, tell me what I need to know before we talk to Avalon, then?"

"They are matriarchal, just like deer. They are skittish and nervous, just like deer. The herd is very shy, and their behavior can sometimes be difficult to predict. Though they feel secure here, the weredeer do live in a place with their natural predators so they never quite relax. You have to deal with them *gently*."

"Even the alpha?"

"*Especially* the alpha. She's the one that warns the herd away from danger. You can lose *dozens* of your best people because of a wrong word that freaks her out," Fiona explained. "You get her to trust you, the herd will trust you. You don't, they'll all hide, or bolt."

"Lovely."

"Right now, you offer them protection, and so

in theory, you have their unwavering loyalty," Fiona said as we walked again. "Just don't say anything that could be interpreted as an inability to protect them."

"Got it."

As we came up to the edge of the canopy, Fiona reached out a hand to slow my approach, and whispered, "Avalon?"

The woman's head snapped toward us like a rubber-band on her neck, and in the blink of an eye, she was on her feet, muscles tense. After a long pause, she relaxed her limbs only slightly. "Yes?"

"Avalon, this is Charlotte Astley. She's the new ringmaster of Magical Midway."

"I know that," Avalon answered softly. Her eyes moved quickly toward me, and back to Fiona.

"I told her how important the weredeer are to the Midway, and Charlotte wanted to come right away to meet the boss of such a talented and accomplished herd. She told me that we had to make absolutely sure you were happy with everything and that you didn't have any concerns about the management change," Fiona said to the nervous woman.

Your friend lies like a champion, Samson thought toward me.

Didn't some people think kelpies were demons, historically? Heck, are kelpies demons? I asked him.

Best not to ask too many questions like that, Samson thought back. *Just remember, even paranormal creatures evolve.*

I gulped.

"We're fine," Avalon responded as she flicked her eyes to me and then dropped them shyly. I nodded and smiled at the timid woman.

"I'm so glad," I told her warmly, taking extraordinary care to keep my words soft. Which wasn't something easy for me. I was kind of loud and direct. "I want to make sure that everyone will be staying on, and there's nothing I can do for you."

"You'll do nothing for us?" The weredeer woman's eyes grew wide and panicky, and she stepped back into the chair she had just been sitting on. It fell back with a thud, startling her even more.

"That's not what I meant!" I protested and stepped toward her. Aggressively, I realized too late. I had raised my voice and stepped toward her aggressively. Which was stupid. A dumb, foolish move. That Fiona warned me about. And which I did anyway.

Because I'm an idiot.

In the time I took to freeze my advance, the terrified woman was gone. She exited the area so quickly that I didn't even see her go.

Fiona stared at me, mouth agape. Silently, she raised her palms to either side of my head and flicked my ears in a most humiliating manner.

"Human. Air. Between. The ears," she said with each flick of her finger.

"What now—never mind, I know. Ask the cat."

Samson rubbed his face against my ankle and sneezed.

"What did you *do* to me, *Ringmaster?*" Dergal accused loudly as he stepped up on Fiona and me, banging into me so hard that I dropped the tumbler my mother had given me. We had been walking around the Midway searching for the place that the weredeer had withdrawn to, when the angry centaur approached.

If they *were* anywhere close, they no doubt bolted when they heard Dergal's booming anger.

"Hello, Dergal," I said in as friendly a voice as I could muster toward a tall, muscled, bitter man that would put his hands on someone like Alessandra. Samson leaned his lithe body against my calf and wound himself around my legs while Fiona stared at Dergal silently. "Just a little protection spell."

"I can take care of myself," he argued as he leaned over and grabbed my tumbler off the ground. "I don't *need* a protection spell, so you can take this garbage from me *right now*."

"I can't really do that."

"Of course you can. You're the ringmaster. *Do it!*"

"Don't give me orders, Dergal," I snapped, losing my patience with him. Vague energy of approval surged quickly from my familiar even as Dergal advanced on me. "And you are right, I am *capable* of taking this off of you. I am *choosing* not to do so at this time."

"You stupid, uppity—"

"What's going on here?" Ningul, the centaur leader, asked as he walked over to the four of us in front of the Haunted House where he worked. "Dergal, this is no way to speak to the ringmaster! My apologies, Ringmaster."

"She's wrapped me in some kind of protection

spell! I can't do any of my work or hit anything with a hammer! I can't even peel an orange!" The frustrated centaur shoved my tumbler back at me aggressively.

We may have been too vehement with that protection spell, Samson thought. *Perhaps we should have been more specific about what he could and could not harm.*

You know, Samson, I'm not feeling particularly guilty about going a bit overboard, I responded. *In fact, I'm enjoying his lousy day just a little bit more than I should be.*

You are the ringmaster, Samson snickered. *I'm happy to follow your lead here.*

"Maybe we should take this conversation off the public thoroughfare and discuss the situation someplace that has a little more privacy?" I suggested as I noticed faces turning to watch the scene.

Ningul nodded, and we walked toward the Haunted House. Dergal followed reluctantly, his hands balled into fists and his face taut with anger.

Entering the front hallway of the Haunted House, I was delighted at the fancy Victorian decor, despite the tense situation. The reception area had lovely antique sofas against every wall, and we all took a seat.

"Ningul, I have placed a protection spell around Dergal due to an accusation of aggression that resulted in injury, as well as some concern that he might be involved in the murder of my uncle."

"Murder!" Ningul appeared shocked at my suggestion while Dergal slammed back on the velvet loveseat and slapped his knee as he sneered at me. "There must be some mistake."

"There may be a mistake," I told him, and a quick check of Ningul's energy indicated extreme shock at my statement. I didn't have any reason to believe Ningul knew anything about what Dergal may have done, but now I felt more comfortable trusting him.

"We're currently trying to investigate so we can get the full picture of what happened. Dergal has denied being at the weredeer party, as well as taking the drink that we know poisoned my uncle from Jeannie to my uncle. Jeannie, however, is clear that Dergal had the cup."

"Wait a minute. I was at that party. I saw Dergal several times." Ningul turned to the younger centaur. "Why did you tell them you weren't there?"

"I don't owe her any explanation for anything I do," Dergal scoffed.

"She's the ringmaster, Dergal."

"Women are *not* ringmasters. When we get a *real* ringmaster, I'll answer *his* questions. We're centaurs. We don't answer to mere women of *any* species," Dergal said furiously.

Ningul stared at Dergal's smug face as if he had grown a second head. The centaur leader's strong hands ran through his dark hair nervously as the two men's eyes locked on one another. After a time, Ningul turned his attention back to me.

"First, I need to apologize again for young Dergal's disrespect. I am mortified that one of my own would speak to you in such a manner," Ningul said. "It seems we have been quite lax in teaching the newer generation some of our histories. I promise you that I will rectify that."

"It happens," I told the centaur. "I'm not as wrapped up in all this formality, but, frankly, he shouldn't be talking like that to any woman. It's what he said that concerns me more than who he said it to."

"I understand, Ringmaster."

"Please, call me Charlotte. I really do get uncomfortable with all this formality," I told

Ningul. He nodded. "In addition to the problems he's causing with the investigation into my uncle's murder, he put his hands on Alessandra. I saw her this morning, and there were bruises up and down her arms."

"You told me that she was sick and you were carrying her home!" Ningul exploded toward Dergal. The powerful man stood up and planted himself in front of the younger centaur. "You don't put bruises on a woman that you are attempting to ensure will get home safe!" Dergal fixed his dark eyes on his leader and flexed the fists at his sides, but wisely said nothing.

"Mark Botsworth, the mentalist, interceded between them. I haven't talked to him yet, but until I do, I want to make sure that Dergal is unable to hurt anyone else."

"I agree, and I thank you for preventing this young colt from engaging in any more of his arrogant stupidity! You will tell the ringmaster the truth! Now!" Ningul roared at Dergal.

I flinched, and Ningul wasn't even yelling at me. Angry centaurs were terrifying to behold.

Dergal exploded out of his chair and raised his arm to hit the older centaur, but his fist harmlessly bounced off Ningul's chin with the now familiar metallic clunk. Dergal roared, turning to slam his body through the exit door.

"Cornered animals are rarely easy to deal with, Ningul," Fiona told the centaur leader quietly. Ningul sank down on the love seat and buried his face in his hands. She got up and went to sit beside him, resting a comforting hand on his back. "Those of a horse nature most of all. You cannot control the herd. You can only lead them and hope that they follow."

"Our last leader, he was a strong man. But he believed that, like the centaurs of old, our bestial nature should be allowed reign over our civilized nature more often than I felt was healthy. He allowed wine once a moon. When he passed, and I became the leader, I stopped that." Fiona nodded while I listened with fascination.

"Why don't you allow the centaurs to drink wine?" I asked.

"Alcohol drives us mad. We become aggressive, demanding, with desires to fight and conquer others. We have evolved over time, and so the madness is not what it once was," he told me. "But it seems the madness has evolved as well. Young Dergal drinks too much wine. I could smell it on him here. His attitude, his aggression…It is a form of centaur madness."

"See, Charlotte, each paranormal creature has something akin to an Achilles heel. Some herb or food or drink that can throw them back into their natures of old," Fiona told me as she continued to distractedly stroke the brokenhearted Ningul's arm gently.

"As a witch, you have a sensitivity to henbane," Ningul explained. "It will pop you right out of your body and allow you to walk your spirit with ease. It takes only a tiny amount, but too much, and it will separate your spirit from your body forever."

"For everyone else, henbane makes us feel like we're flying, or drunk, or can sedate us, so we're happily barely conscious if we have an injury. It's also *awesome* if you have a toothache," Fiona said.

"That's good to know. Although I don't know where anyone would get henbane."

"Any apothecary, even in the human world," Ningul said. "Though it's not as common as wine, which is our current problem."

"Humans will sell *anything*, even if it's toxic," Fiona said.

"Yeah, yeah, yeah, I know, bad humans. Blah, blah, blah. Let's get back to the issue at hand. If Dergal's not going to tell us the truth, how do we figure this out?" Fiona and Ningul stared at me in expectation.

You are the ringmaster, Samson said. *They are waiting for you to tell them what's going to happen.*

"Maybe it's time to talk to Mark Botsworth," I announced. "I'd like to know what he saw." They nodded.

It's good to be king, hmmm? Samson said.

CHAPTER 9

As we stepped into the sunshine in front of the Haunted House, Ningul let us know that he would go look for Dergal. Though the angry centaur could harm no one physically, he was unhinged, and Ningul wanted to protect others from him, and him from himself. As the three of us spoke quietly at the bottom of the stairs, a shimmery head poked through the closed door above us.

Like, *through* the door. A head, right through the door. It was a man, handsome, with an old-fashioned haircut and spectacles.

"Excuse me, Ringmaster?" the voice called.

"What. Is. That?" I asked Fiona.

"One of the ghosts. In the Haunted House?" If

Fiona didn't stop looking at me like I was daft, I swore to myself I would sneak up on her in her pen and put a knot in her darn tail that no one would ever get out.

"So. I'm sure this is a dumb question. But I'm going to ask it anyway. We have *real* ghosts living in the Haunted House?"

"Of course we do," Ningul answered as he raised an eyebrow toward Fiona. No one at this damn place seemed to bother with the effort to be furtive about their shock at my ignorance. "What did you *think* was in the Haunted House?"

"Um, animatronics? Like at Disney World?"

"Oh, please. Like those aren't *real* ghosts at Disney World," the ghost head still hanging out of the door said. "Ringmaster, I just wanted to let you know that you left your black drink tumbler in here."

"I don't think that's mine. Mine's silver not… black…" Slowly remembering my mother's reason for giving it to me, I raced up the stairs and threw the door open—walking right through the ghost man. Which was about as creepy as you would think.

Next to where I had been sitting was the tumbler my mother had given me. It had changed color from the bright silver to a dark and ominous black. Pulling off the lid, I could see dark grains of something floating in the water.

Fiona, who had raced up behind me, stared into the cup in shock. "But I could swear he was never near your glass! He sat next to Ningul the whole time!"

Ningul, who had followed Fiona, fell to his knees and bowed his head, begging for mercy. "Please, Ringmaster, do not slaughter the entire herd because of one young stallion's folly! I *beg* of you, Ringmaster, do not kill us all!"

The hallway instantly filled with ghosts popping into place. The crowd seemed to take up every available space in the reception area, murmuring and exclaiming as they watched Ningul on his knees with concern.

"Oh, my gosh, could everyone just stop a minute!" I shouted as the din of ghosts chattered, Ningul begged, and Fiona hyperventilated. The chaos of panic squeezed out any rational, cognizant thought I might have been able to have. "Just calm down, everyone!"

Why is Ningul on his knees? I practically shouted in my head at Samson.

If someone is caught trying to murder a new ringmaster within the first moon of their reign, every member of that guilty species is killed. The shared responsibility is supposed to protect the new ringmaster while they are getting to know their new position, Samson explained.

Oh, for heaven's sake. Who came up with that insane idea?

Ringmaster number three.

So, do I have to follow that rule? Samson paused as he thought about my question.

No, Samson said.

"Ningul, no one's going to slaughter any herd of anything. Get up," I told him as I reached down and pulled the large, sexy, muscled man from his knees. "Now, all of you ghosts—did any of you see anything? Did you see the cup turn from silver to black at any point?"

"No, Ringmaster," one ghost said. The other spirits quietly chimed in that they, too, had seen nothing.

"The tumbler was black when you came to visit," a young shimmering girl told me. "I know it was because I was watching out the window upstairs even though Mama tells me I shouldn't watch the window. But I was, and I thought it was pretty how your cup matched Samson."

"What's your name, honey?" I asked the tiny ghost as I walked over to her.

"Anna. My Mom is over there," she pointed

cheerfully. Her shimmering mother smiled and bowed her head in my direction.

"How old are you, Anna?"

"Two hundred and fifty-seven!" she told me proudly. I stared at the girl.

"Ringmaster," Anna's mother stepped up and wrapped a ghostly arm around her daughter. "Anna was five when she and I passed on from the material world in a house fire. Five she was and five she will always be." I stepped over and squatted down so the ghostly little girl and I could gaze at each other eye to...um, eye likeness.

"Well, for a little girl, Anna, you did a *crackerjack* job. That was important information, thank you." I bumped my forehead toward hers, and she giggled as the edges of her visage broke apart and fogged around my eyes.

"Mama, the ringmaster said I did a good job!" Anna told her mother proudly. The matronly ghost leaned down and swooped up the image of her daughter and hugged her. "I did, Mama, I did! Am I in trouble now? For looking out the window? And what's a crackerjack?"

"No, sweetheart," her mother answered. The little girl beamed.

"So, Dergal didn't do it here. It doesn't mean he didn't do it at all," Fiona observed as she stared at the offending tumbler. I capped it again and sighed. "Be careful with that, Charlotte. If you forget and drink that, you'll be dead. And meaning no offense, but we're fast running out of eligible ringmasters."

"I am *not* going to the Makepeace Circus," one ghost said. "That man is just as uppity as those other witches in the towns. That place is horrible. Horrible!"

"Protect the ringmaster!" another ghost shouted, and the assembled thirty or so spirits suddenly converged on me. Like a wriggling, seething shield, they formed a ghostly egg that must have appeared very much like the shimmering cocoon I saw in Samson's visions.

Except this one had over thirty faces, sixty arms, and legs, and dropped the temperature of the air around my body at least fifty degrees in an instant. My hands felt like ice, and my teeth chattered as the assembled ghosts shouted and cheered themselves on.

"W-w-while I ap-p-preciate the sentiment," I said as my breath blew white into the cool air and I struggled to move within my impromptu ghost body-wrap, "p-p-please g-get away from m-me. I'm f-f-freezing to d-death. I won't n-need to worry ab-b-bout poison."

It was as if they hadn't heard me. The ghosts didn't move.

My lungs felt as if a weight was pressing down on them, a brick of ice squeezing all the oxygen from my body. As I pleaded with them to back away, the chattering grew more pronounced, and I began violently shivering.

Enough of this, Samson thought. *Light flashed, and ghosts flew away from me in every direction. A balmy yellow glow surrounded me, and I felt my body warm. You must learn how to use your magic. If you die of something as silly as ghost-induced hypothermia, I will never live it down.*

Thank you, I sent him as I warmed up. The hypothermia and the warming seemed to take place at a pace far faster than it would have been in the human world. Everything in the paranormal world seemed to somehow be magnified—magnified benefits, amplified consequences.

"Again, I appreciate the sentiment," I said once I could speak without chattering my words. "But I have my own defenses. I promise you guys, I'll be okay."

Speaking of which, my automatic defenses didn't seem to help, Samson. What gives?

You can still feel the weather, Samson said. *I don't*

know that the concept of a ringmaster wandering about the Alaskan tundra in their skivvies was an attack anyone ever considered crafting a defense for.

"You know, your uncle gave us all those same assurances," Fiona said as she hugged me. "Don't get too cocky."

Considering poison and extreme temperatures could kill me, the amazing indestructible ringmaster, I had to wonder what other limits just hadn't been tested enough to know that they would fail.

I nodded at Fiona and worried.

As I walked into the communications yurt, I threw the black tumbler across the room in frustration. In my first afternoon as the new ringmaster, I had frightened all the weredeer, nearly been poisoned, almost been frozen, ticked off my familiar, made up with my familiar, and had to deal with the emotional roller coaster of people thinking I was a murderous tyrant or inept.

That doesn't even count the Magical Midway's capital and domestic crime problem.

And now I had no water again.

My one-week visits to the Magical Midway had not been remotely enough to comprehend the intricacies of this world. I didn't even know if things were like this because of the paranormal world at large or if all this weirdness was limited to the paranormal circuses. If it was all paranormal places, there might not be much I could do about it.

If it was just my circus, I had to fix it.

Come to think of it, if it was just the circuses, I was starting to comprehend *why* there were only two left. This was a job more significant than any one person should ever have to have.

Hard afternoon? my uncle asked from a seat in the corner.

"Where the heck have you been? And *how* did you do this?" I asked him as I walked across the room to pick up the tumbler I had just thrown. There was possibly poison in it.

"Everyone is so emotional, and all these old rules have no place in the modern world. Everyone seems to be struggling with something or angry about something or afraid of something. And I'm afraid to think something too strongly lest I relocate us to Mars! Uncle Phil, I honestly don't know if I'm cut out for this," I told him as I sat down next to him.

Ah, the first stage of grief. Uncle Phil smiled at me. *It's the moment that the excitement begins to wear off and you suddenly comprehend that this place is just a little bit crazy, and you are now the mayor of crazy town.*

"That's *not* funny," I told him as I struggled not to crack up. A tiny chuckle escaped my lips. Uncle Phil smiled a little bit. Then I giggled. Then he laughed. Finally, my uncle and I were laughing so hard tears rolled down my cheeks, and he twinkled with little fireworks.

As our laughter subsided, Uncle Phil cleared his throat. *I do understand what you're going through. Whether it's a human circus or paranormal circus, people that choose this life are either running away from something or are searching for something that they're having trouble finding. Either way, they are a different breed. It means that you have a bigger task, a greater responsibility, and until you understand them you will likely have a tougher time.*

"Dergal came at me today, and when we found the poison in my cup, we assumed that he had done it. Ningul was there when we found out, and he was so frightened of me that it freaked me out. Anya mentioned I get to decide whether people live or die," I sighed and rubbed my eyes. "I just…man."

The ringmaster does have ultimate power over the Magical Midway, Uncle Phil said. He reached out to squeeze my knee, but his hand just passed through my limb. Sighing, my uncle patted the air above it. It wasn't that comforting.

"I don't think I like having all this power, Uncle Phil. I don't know that *anyone* should have this much power. I'm less afraid of being poisoned than I am of being put in a situation where I have to decide whether someone gets to live or die."

You arrived at that conclusion earlier than most of us.

"Wait a minute…you think ringmasters are too powerful?"

Of course we are. We have all the talents, all the powers, and all the abilities. If we took the time to learn all that we could do, we would possibly be invincible. Our only saving grace is that most of us, once we discover just how much power we have, choose not to use most of those abilities or test its bounds. We learn what we decide we need to know and leave the rest alone.

I nodded. "Then why do we still have it?"

What are we going to do with it?" he asked, waving his arms in the air. *It has to go somewhere. Do you give it to someone? Do you dissipate it into thin air, leaving all the residents here unprotected? Do you limit it permanently, not knowing whether you will need what you have limited, to save someone's life? And if you did, would that limitation even stick?"*

I didn't know. I took some comfort in the fact that evidently no one else, did, either. The Magical Midway seemed to be all or nothing. Despite its name, there really was no middle way for it to survive.

It's a hard question, my girl. Perhaps you will be the ringmaster that figures it out.

I shook my head. "Right now I can't even figure out how to solve your murder. Heck, I can't even talk to the weredeer. I scared them off. The whole herd is hiding somewhere."

Anya actually went and talked to them for you, Uncle Phil told me. *That girl may seem tough as nails, but she and Avalon are close friends. She was able to explain what was going on, so they are all back at their posts. Crisis averted.*

"Anya and Avalon. Close friends. Combat boots Anya and meek, skittish Avalon are friends?"

They are, quite close, Uncle Phil said. *Things are not always as they appear, and people are not all that they seem. Especially here. In any case, Anya has interceded for you, though you will still need to stop by at some point and formalize your protection for Avalon.*

I breathed a sigh of relief. "I'm so glad. I felt bad. I didn't mean to scare her."

Charlotte, I promise you that it does get better. I know it feels like I haven't helped you very much with this, but there is a reason for that. Samson will be there for you to make sure that you don't do anything too terrible, but I want you to decide for yourself what type of ringmaster you will be, Uncle Phil admitted. *I don't want to unduly influence you, or force you into the mold I followed.*

"Did Grandpa let you find your own way?"

Oh goodness, no, Uncle Phil laughed. *He cast his eyes around the room as if expecting to see his father manifest next to his chair. My father was a strict man. He believed that sternness was necessary for the safety of the Magical Midway. I don't know that he was wrong, at least in his time.*

"Yeah, maybe." I leaned back in the chair.

It's only in the past ten years or so, Charlotte, that I truly came into my own as the ringmaster. I wasted many years trying to be my father, trying to do it the way I believed he would want me to. Dad stayed to train me full-time for three years, and it took me ten more to realize I didn't always have to do it exactly the way he wanted me to.

"Wow. Do you wish that he hadn't stayed?"

Trying to get rid of me so fast, dear girl? My uncle looked shocked and hurt and the suggestion, but then he winked. I rolled my eyes. Even in death, Uncle Phil had to be a comedian. After a few moments, my uncle's expression turned serious.

I wish he hadn't tried to make me into him, Uncle Phil said at the end of a long pause. *I wish he had worked with me to find the best way for me. I am trying to make sure that in guiding you, we find the best way for you.*

"Thanks, Uncle Phil. I would give you a hug, but I'm afraid with the way my day has been going I would just fall through you and break my nose." We both laughed, and he blew me a kiss the way he used to do when I was a small child.

Call your mother. You need some dinner. With no henbane—which is, incidentally, what's in that tumbler of yours. I've worked with it enough to recognize the grains.

I nodded and got up reluctantly. I wasn't looking forward to using the calling cauldron, though my mother's promised dinner and pie were making my mouth water. When I handed her the black tumbler back and asked for another, she would lose it. One more hysterical, emotional person was the last thing I needed.

Not enough to avoid the call, not eat, and give up the pie, mind you. But still. Not looking forward to it.

~

A Costco apple pie.

Besides the traditional dinner of meatloaf, mashed potatoes, broccoli, and a roll, my mother shoved an entire Costco apple pie through the mist as a treat.

An *entire* lattice-covered Costco apple pie.

Before I had got the pie, however, my mother had extracted every last bit of information out of me regarding the situation at the Magical Midway. She had a typical Mom meltdown, but eventually, I repeated enough assurances and promises that everyone and everything would be all right.

At least enough she would hand over the darn pie.

Okay, I may have fibbed a little.

There are few things in the human world better than Costco baked goods. Well, there probably are, but I didn't get out much. We shopped at Costco a whole lot, thanks to the animals at the shelter needing an awful lot of stuff in bulk, and Costco's pizza slice was always a treat.

But nothing beat a Costco apple pie.

"This is fantastic pie," Fiona mumbled as the crust dribbled from her lips and bounced off her shirt. The pies are enormous, so I invited Fiona and Fortuna to share in the bounty. I couldn't let any of it sit around waiting for the poisoner. "I think I love your mom, Charlotte."

"Yes, thank you," Fortuna said as she shoveled in an extra large portion of the extra large piece of the extra large pie. "I haven't had one of these in many years, and yet it doesn't seem to have changed."

"I love sundown around here," I sighed and gazed out the screened window at the beautiful orange-red sky. The sun was seconds away from slipping below the horizon, and bright stars were winning their fight to shine. "Everything feels so peaceful, even though it isn't."

"As soon as the dark comes, things will be decidedly less peaceful and quiet, ay?" Fiona said as Fortuna laughed and nodded.

"Oh no. No. What's going on? What's wrong now?"

"Nothing's wrong, your highness," Fiona laughed. "The Midway will be celebrating your arrival tonight—it's not every day that we get a new ringmaster. Did your uncle not tell you about the party?"

I shook my head no.

"Perhaps he wanted to surprise you," Fortuna said as she shifted in her chair and placed her empty plate on the coffee table in the seating area. "A ringmaster change typically only happens once a generation. A new one coming heralds a future for the Magical Midway, and so people wish to celebrate that. It's an old, old tradition."

"Is there some magical ritual or something I need to know about?"

"No, this is all informal. The leaders of each clan or group will come and introduce themselves. I have to ask, Charlotte—what did you think all that activity was under the Big Top?"

"Well, we *are* a circus. I figured we were going to open at some point to people and everyone was getting ready."

Nothing will open to humans for three days after you take over, Samson said. *We couldn't open it if we wanted to. Humans cannot cross the barrier until the full moon.*

You guys really never thought of writing all this down?

No need. I'm aware of it all.

Except for the freezing to death thing.

Now I'm aware of it.

Anything else I need to be aware of? I asked him.

Roland Makepeace is likely to make an appearance at the party to greet you. Beyond that, this is just a party in the middle of a murder investigation and a potential assassination attempt. Nothing to worry about. Just don't eat or drink anything.

"At a party? Come on," I said as I got up to gather the plates. "Aren't we reasonably sure Dergal is behind this? Is this all still necessary? Honestly, I grabbed dinner from my Mom mostly because of the promise of pie."

Reasonably sure is not entirely sure, Samson pointed out. *Ningul is trying to sober up the wayward stallion, but we have no guarantee he's not a murderer without the alcohol. He may not confess.*

"Great," I mumbled. "A party where I can't eat or drink. Sounds awesome." I placed the stacked plates on the cauldron and turned back to Fiona and Fortuna. Both of whom were staring at me with looks of total perplexity on their faces.

"The cat," I said and waived in Samson's direction. Fiona raised an eyebrow.

"I thought I could hear the cat?"

"I made a mistake," I told her as our eyes met,

hoping she would not pry any further into my screwup. Fiona's head tilted to the side, and she opened her mouth as if to say something. After a glance at Samson, she snapped her mouth shut and smiled.

"All fixed, I'm sure," Fiona smiled and took another bite out of her pie.

Anya burst into the tent heaving in immense gasps. Clutching my arm, she panted. "My sister is gone! I left for just an hour to talk to Avalon, and when I came back she was gone!"

Fiona and Fortuna jumped from their seats and helped Anya to a chair so she could catch her breath. "Go get Ningul," I said to Fiona. "Find out if he still has Dergal or if Dergal's missing, too." She nodded and quickly left the yurt.

"She swore that she would stay in the room," Anya snarled. "She's so mercurial sometimes, though. I don't know what goes through her head! Even though that stupid glue factory candidate hurt her, she just keeps going back to him!"

I winced at the glue factory comment and was grateful that Fiona had left the immediate area.

"We'll find her, Anya. The grounds aren't really that big," I told the bristle-headed siren.

"Why do you think Alessandra went back to Dergal?"

The fiery woman slapped the arms on the chair and thrust herself back with a thwack. "She thinks she loves that complete jerk. I wish she would just do the water test on him and be done with it already."

"The water test?" I stared from Fortuna to Anya. "What's the water test?"

"We are water nymphs," Anya said, leaning forward. "We can bring men near water and call to them with our song. If they are pure of heart and do not have a stain on their soul, they will simply come to us as if in a dream. If they mean us harm or are of evil character, they will drown themselves in the water."

"Oh dear. Those are the only two possible outcomes of the song?"

"Once heard, yes," Anya nodded. "So, you generally want to be really sure they're good. Or, you know, really sure they're bad. Depending on what you want the outcome to be. Either way, though, it is their choice and their responsibility, really. They don't have to be unicorn dung."

Can I magically keep this from happening? I asked Samson.

No, Samson responded. *Your magic cannot*

*change the magical nature of any paranormal creature
or limit the magic inherent in their species. That
would violate their paranormal rights to be who
they are.*

I thought you said I was practically omnipotent?

Practically omnipotent, Samson replied.
*Practically would be the critical word in that
statement. Your only choice would be to banish Dergal
or Alessandra, or both. That would not stop it from
happening, it would just prevent it from happening*
here. *It would also upset the centaurs and the naiads.*

My Uncle Phil wasn't kidding when he said
this was like being the mayor of crazy town. With
each power I uncovered, a limitation or
consideration popped up to go with it that
seemed to directly counter my ability to avert a
potential catastrophe.

Even though my feet were firmly on the
ground, I felt like I was walking a tightrope.

CHAPTER 10

As Fiona returned with a concerned-looking Ningul just moments later, Anya exploded out of her chair toward the handsome centaur leader. "Your horse-man has done enough damage to my sister! Where is he? What has he done with her?" Anger flashed across his chiseled face as the siren flew at him.

"I have placed Dergal in our containment residence until he sobers up. He has done nothing to your sister, Anya," Ningul told her calmly. She hovered angrily just inches from his face. "I just left him sleeping off his sober-up coffee from Hildegaard's. If you cannot find your sister, it is not young Dergal's doing. Now step off, nymph."

Ningul stared at the furious young woman, but she did not back up.

"Folks, how about everyone take a deep breath and calm down?" I said as I slipped my hands between them and palmed their torsos to push them apart.

What the hell do the Larry brothers even do here, Samson? This is the third time I could have used security, and they're nowhere around when I need them.

They're patrolling. There's only five of them. They can't be everywhere all at once. Besides, you can't be physically hurt, so what do you care? Get in there, Rocky.

Right, unless someone throws an ice cube at me. How do you know about the movie Rocky?

I know much more than you think I do, Samson thought haughtily.

And yet not as much as I wish you did, I shot back.

Touché, Samson reluctantly admitted.

"Look, I understand that everyone is worried. Ningul, you are worried about Dergal—"

"I am not worried *about* that pile of elephant manure. I can't stand that young man. I'm worried *about* what that glorified donkey will do next that will bring shame down on my herd." I stared at the centaur leader in surprise. "What? Just because I have to lead the centaurs doesn't mean I have to like all of them."

"Let's start with the premise that I'm not gonna slaughter all of the centaurs if Dergal is a jerk that hits girls and poisons ringmasters," I told Ningul matter-of-factly.

"If we start with that premise and I *promise* not to hold you responsible for his actions just because you're the leader, can you tell me honestly about Dergal? How long has he been here? Why do you dislike him? Do *you* think that he tried to kill my Uncle Phil?"

"Dergal arrived about four years ago," Ningul began as he carefully stepped away from Anya and moved to take a seat on a rattan chair. "I was not that impressed with the young stallion from the get-go, but he had no history in the centaur world that would indicate I had a particular reason to refuse him."

"Did you ever ask his old herd if he hit women?" Anya snarled. I placed a hand gently on the angry naiad's shoulder. She whirled on me ready to fight, and then slumped back toward the centaur. "I am sorry. You didn't hit my sister, and I have known you some years, Ningul. Had you known, I am sure you would've stepped in to stop what was happening to her."

"I *have* stepped in, Anya," Ningul said as he turned to her. "I have had to step in with Dergal and various women over and over again. Women that he lied to, women that he cheated on, women that wanted to carve him up into horse-meat roasts for the way he treated them. I never thought, though, that he would raise a hand to anyone. I believe the drink brought the worst out in him. I wish I had realized sooner."

"Ningul, you are a new leader," Fiona told him gently as she knelt beside him and placed a hand on his. "It takes many years of practice and many failures to make a good leader. Don't be too hard on yourself."

Ningul and Fiona gazed into each other's eyes. If her gaze filled with any more affection and admiration, it would spill out of her and melt her darn clothes off. I groaned to myself as I recognized yet another complication rearing its head and whinnying.

"Hey, folks, I appreciate the support, but I'd like to be able to eat food at the Midway at some point," I broke into their mutual admiration society rudely. "Again, do we think that Dergal could have poisoned Uncle Phil?"

"As much as I dislike him, I cannot see what reason he would have to poison your uncle, or you, Charlotte," Ningul said as he tore his eyes away from Fiona still kneeling beside him. "The boy is stupid, reckless, and sometimes quite mean, but murder? I don't think I can see it."

"Anyone that would hit a woman or grab her and drag her hard enough to leave bruises is capable of anything. Violence is violence," Anya disagreed.

"Poison is not aggression," Fiona pointed out. "Poison is conniving and sneaky."

"Cheating on a woman and lying to her isn't conniving or sneaky?" Anya exploded. "I can't think of anything more conniving or sneaky!"

"But Dergal is clearly getting something that he wants out of that," Fiona countered. "The fact that he dates multiple women and pretends to the women that he's not is *because* he wants multiple women. What would he get out of killing the ringmaster? If both ringmasters die, what happens to the Magical Midway?"

At the moment, you would likely pass on the Midway to your father, Samson interjected in my mind.

"Okay, if I died, I would pick my father, but

what if he was murdered? What then?" I hated even asking the question out loud.

There would be no one left, Samson said. *The Magical Midway would cease to be. Without a bloodline to carry on the magic, the Magical Midway would be no more.*

"Is there any reason that Dergal would want the Magical Midway to disappear?" I asked the group. Silence descended as the suggestion shocked all assembled. They each examined one another as if they were searching for an answer in the face of someone else. "So, who benefits if the Midway disappears?"

"The Makepeace Circus," Fiona chimed in. "They could take some of the acts from the Magical Midway that they've been wanting. Roland Makepeace would also be the only bloodline power left."

"The Witches' Council," Anya added. "Everyone knows the Witches' Council wishes that all of the circuses and fairs would just disappear off the face of the earth."

"All of this has always been true, though," I pointed out to the group. "None of these reasons are new. Different circuses wanted better acts than they had, the Witches' Council can't stand any of us…I mean, all those things have been true for generations. So, why now?"

Everyone grew quiet and thought intently about what might have changed in the paranormal world that would make the destruction of the Magical Midway imperative to someone. No one could come up with anything.

"Does your uncle have any ideas?" Fiona asked.

"I haven't seen him for a while." I scanned the corners of the communications tent in case I had missed his bright rainbow colored sparkle. Nope. He definitely wasn't around.

Do you know where Uncle Phil is?

He has been spending time in Jeannie's Snack Shop, Samson admitted. *She is so upset about what happened to him. Your uncle feels very guilty about leaving her.*

"He's busy at the moment," I told them. "I'll ask him when I see him again."

"I feel like we're missing something," Fiona said.

"We are—we are missing Alessandra!" Anya told her as she stomped on the ground.

"I don't mean a person, I mean we're missing some piece of information. I think we need to talk to Mark Botsworth. He saw whatever happened between Alessandra and Dergal. I'd like to know exactly what it is that he saw."

"I'm coming with you," Anya said.

"I as well," Fortuna said quietly. I jumped, shocked that she was still in the room. The tiny woman in the layers of peasant shirts and skirts had been astoundingly quiet during all the interesting interaction. "I came with Mark from the Langdon Circus, so I know him. It would likely be more comfortable for him to see a friendly face."

"I have a friendly face!" Anya argued as she balled her fists up.

"Very friendly," I assured her. "But Fortuna's right. Let's make sure he doesn't feel like the cavalry is coming to attack him." She would also be useful if Mark Botsworth turned out to be less than forthcoming.

We left Ningul in the skillful hands of the consoling Fiona, and I did my best not to roll my eyes on our way out.

As Anya, Fortuna, and I stepped out of the communications yurt and began the short walk toward the mentalist's stick joint, we walked smack into a gigantic, jiggling giant of a man.

"Well, I can sense the new ringmaster standing right in front of me!" the man bellowed as he grabbed my hand roughly and pumped it while slapping my shoulder. "Power speaks to power, little girl, and I can certainly feel yours struggling to wrap itself around you. Doesn't *quite* fit, does it?"

Little girl. Oh, *great*. A man that thinks a nearly thirty-year-old woman should be classified as a child. What is it with the paranormal world and misogyny?

I yanked my hand from his and stepped back. The man had all the earmarks of a ringmaster on a 1920s circus poster. With a black top hat, red jacket, white shirt, black pants, and shiny black boots, he was the picture of a ringmaster stereotype. His handlebar mustache came out two inches into the air just under his chubby apple cheeks. His smile, however, didn't reach his eyes and I was immediately on guard.

"Dad, do you have to talk like you're in some 1950s circus drama? Ms. Astley, I am Gunther Makepeace, and this is my father, Roland Makepeace. We traveled here to introduce ourselves. My father is the current ringmaster of the Makepeace Family Circus." Gunther Makepeace stepped forward politely and extended his hand, waiting for me to take it. I did, and we shook firmly but gently.

"It's nice to meet you, Gunther. Please, call me Charlotte," I answered. Gunther's hair was the lightest of blond, and his eyes were a deep emerald green. He was at least six inches taller than I was, and his physique rivaled the centaurs. There was something about him, some energy that made me feel instantly at ease.

As opposed to his father, who repulsed me. Just a little.

"Now that we've got that out of the way, little girl, tell me how much would you like to sell the Magical Midway for?" Roland Makepeace said as he pushed his son out of the way. Gunther lowered his eyes and shook his head. "Surely a civilized girl like you doesn't want to be stuck running a run-down place like this."

"Mr. Makepeace, as you can tell, I *am* running a place like this. I have no interest in selling. I don't even know how you would sell something like…this place."

"Well, you would take the money, and we would take the circus. And your cat, of course."

Don't you have anything to say about this jerk? I

thought to Samson. Without answering, Samson leaped to my shoulder and settled in like a parrot. As he purred, a tiny head peeked out of Gunther's pocket to stare at him.

"No, Delilah, go back in the pocket. Go on, sweetie," Gunther said as he tapped the tiny kitten down.

"Your familiar is named Delilah? I mean, it *is* your familiar, right?"

"Yes," Gunther left as he patted his pocket. "When she first showed up she would sleep on the top of my pillow and lick my head. She also chewed on my hair. So I thought Delilah was a good name for her."

"Samson," I said as I pointed to my shoulder.

"Your familiar—his name is *Samson?*" Gunther asked, laughing.

"I kid you not. Samson and Delilah. What a weird coincidence, huh?"

Yes, what a strange coincidence, Samson thought sarcastically.

"Son, the new ringmaster and I have business to discuss," Roland Makepeace told Gunther sternly, shoving him roughly to the side. As his father stepped slightly in front of him again, Gunther winked at me and mouthed *I'm sorry*. I smiled even more broadly.

He's going to be the next ringmaster, Samson warned me. *Don't even think about it.*

I'm not thinking about anything. Gunther is cute, I'll give you that. And he's got a kitten which, no offense to you or anything, is just adorable. And nothing is cuter than a sexy guy with a sweet kitten. But I'm not thinking about anything.

Uh huh, Samson answered unconvincingly.

"Yes, Gunther, your father and I should discuss what price he wants for the Makepeace Circus," I said as Anya stifled a laugh behind me.

"What? Me sell you *our* family circus? Are you *daft*, girl? How horrible! Insulting! Mockery of my family's legacy! I've never been so offended in my life!" The big man huffed and panted his indignation as I struggled to keep a straight face. Since Gunther was standing behind his father, he could laugh silently. Which he did.

"I mean, obviously. *Obviously*, I must be kidding. Clearly, a ringmaster would never consider selling their family legacy! The ancestors would come rushing out of their graves in protest! That would be unheard of, wouldn't it?" I fluttered my eyelashes at the fat man as he caught on to my passive aggressive insult.

"You are *not* a very nice little girl," Ringmaster Makepeace snapped at me. "Gunther, we have done our duty. Let us leave this filthy place with these substandard facilities." The big man turned on his heel and walked toward the entrance like he was dragging the Midway.

"I apologize for my father," Gunther said as he reached out his hand and grabbed mine again. "He really isn't as horrible as he seems. He's from another time. Dad had me very late in life, and sometimes I feel like we are separated by more generations than just one."

"It's okay, really. My uncle was like that. Well, not as bad as that."

"Oh, I'm sure he is still like that," Gunther laughed. "It's only been a day. I knew your uncle. There is no *way* he left you alone with the Midway this fast." I smiled.

"No. No, he hasn't," I answered. Gunther and I continued to clasp hands for no particular reason I could discern. Neither of us seemed uncomfortable that it had gone on too long. I felt like I should want to pull away, and yet I didn't. His hands were soft and warm.

"Anyway, *I* think you are," he said and smiled again.

"I'm what?"

"Nice. You seem like a very nice young woman. I hope I get to see you sometime when my father is not trying to manipulate you into giving up your family legacy," Gunther gave my hand one last squeeze and then let go. He bowed and turned to follow his father down the Midway.

"That boy has one of the tightest—"

"Anya!" Fortuna gasped.

"What? Tightest handshakes! I was gonna say handshakes! What did you think I was gonna say?" Anya exclaimed innocently.

"You were *not* going to say handshakes," Fortuna chastised her. "You weren't watching his tight handshake walk down the Midway in those tight black pants."

"No, I most certainly was not," Anya said as she fanned herself. "I don't think it matters much anyway. Gunther was hard flashing Charlotte but good."

"Hard flashing?" I asked, confused.

"At carnivals, hard flash is the large and expensive-looking prize," Anya explained. "A lot of times, they are absolutely impossible to win. Gunther was looking at *you* like you were hard flash, Charlotte, and he was ready to buy a ticket to play."

I blushed and shook my head no. "You're dreaming. He was just being friendly, trying to cover for his rude dad, I think." I turned back toward the Midway and strained my eyes to see if Gunther was still there. "How would we even call?"

"They *have* cauldrons," Fortuna pointed out. "Besides, that Samson and Delilah thing. I mean, you have to go out with the guy if he asks now."

"You remember how that ended, right? Guys, someone might be trying to kill me. Maybe we should solve that before I worry about dating."

"You know, he's still standing at the edge of the gate watching you," Anya said as she strained her neck and stared toward the entrance.

"He is? Where? I don't see him."

"Made you look!" Anya smiled, laughed, and pointed at me. "You like Gunther! I knew you did!"

"You guys are impossible!"

"Having a girlfriend as a ringmaster is going to be *so much fun!*" Anya smiled as we continued our interrupted walk toward Mark Botsworth's stick joint.

Mark's place had the four sides rolled down signaling the tent was closed, but a light shined from within. I called inside, and shadows played against the light colored canvas of the walls.

"Yes?" A human that seemed…well, more human than Fortuna stuck his head out of the corner. Mark Botsworth would have appeared entirely at home on the greens of a country club in his khaki slacks and white polo shirt. His dark hair was neatly crew cut, and his face was smooth and clean-shaven despite the late hour of the day.

"Hi, Mark, I'm Charlotte Astley. Do you have a few minutes to answer some questions about what you saw going on between Alessandra and Dergal the other night?"

"Sure, but I'm not sure who those people are," he said as he stepped back to make room for the three of us to pass. "Oh, hey, Fortuna."

"Hi, Mark. Charlotte's the new ringmaster of the Magical Midway. I wasn't sure if you'd heard," Fortuna told him as she lightly touched his wrist with her fingers. My eyes narrowed as I watched the connection last for two seconds, and then Mark gave Fortuna a subtle nod.

Well, *that* was suspicious.

Disappointment welled up in me as I eyed Fortuna, but then I realized I knew nothing about their powers or gifts. I didn't know what that could have been, or why, and I *liked* Fortuna.

With all she had riding on staying at the Magical Midway, could she really be part of this conspiracy?

Sometimes just popping off the obvious question could shake something loose. Maybe it wasn't as bad as it looked. So I took the direct route.

"Since I'm new here, I don't really have this subtle inquest thing down, yet. What the heck was that?"

"What was what, Ms. Astley?" Mark asked me quietly as a red flush crept up his neck.

"That. That touch. Fortuna, what's going on here?"

"Mark is a telepath," Fortuna told me as she squeezed Mark's arm. "He's only been here since July, and he only came to the Langdon Carnival in May. The two of you have really only been acquainted with the paranormal world for about the same amount of time, Charlotte. Though yours came in one-week spurts."

"Right. So?"

"So, Mark is new to this. I was simply sending him the information about this meeting that he needed to know. That you are the new ringmaster, what that means, and an overview of the situation. I also told him not to worry or be nervous as you were not here to ask him to leave."

"I'm sorry, ringmaster," Mark told me softly. "Fortuna was trying to help me not offend you, and in doing so, we already offended you."

"I have to tell you, Mark, the fact that anyone is worried about offending me is probably freaking me out more than any actual offense I could be offended by," I told him. "I'm just Charlotte. I'm not a title, I'm a person. And frankly, you and I probably have a lot more in common than I have with anyone else since we were in the human world so long."

"We had an apple pie from a human place called Costco for dinner," Anya told him.

"Pizza, too?" Mark smiled.

"I wish," I told him. "Please don't be nervous. I'm pretty much human. That's how I was raised, anyway."

"All right then," Mark nodded and gestured to the chairs around his tent. "Please, sit down. I'd offer you something to eat, but it sounds like you just had something."

"We're trying to find out what happened with Dergal and Alessandra," I told him as we took a seat. "I understand that you intervened between them when they were having an argument." His face flashed recognition, and he nodded. "Can you tell me about it?"

"Well, the night that your uncle…Anyway, that night I was sitting in here reading a book when I heard someone cry out. I ran outside to check what was going on."

"What time, do you think?" Fortuna asked.

"Oh, it was late," Mark said. "I read before I go to bed."

"You sleep in here?" I asked. Mark nodded. "Why?"

"I, um…no one ever showed me anywhere else. So I assumed that this was mine to work and sleep in," Mark told me. Anya smacked her forehead with her hand. "It's been fine, really."

"Mark, why didn't you tell me?" Fortuna asked.

"I didn't want to be a bother to anyone. In any case, I went outside to check it out. A man and a woman were arguing. The man was big and very angry. He was holding a glass and trying to force the woman to drink." Anya tensed in the seat next to me, and I could feel the anger radiating off of her. "She was crying and pushing his hands away, and he was grabbing her very roughly."

"Did he force her to drink?"

"He managed to get some of the drink in her, I

think, but I…well, I know I am not supposed to get physical with anyone on the Midway, but I just couldn't watch that. I went and pushed him away from her. The woman ran toward the boat ride, and the man yelled at me for interfering."

"Do you know who the man was?"

"No, I'm sorry," Mark apologized. "I realized when the woman was running back toward the boat ride that she was one of the women that worked there, the blonde woman. I followed and saw her run beneath the waterfall."

"Did the man say anything that would indicate why he was trying to force her to drink something?" Fortuna asked him.

"He was shouting at her that he wanted her to drink so she would stay out of his way and that it was her own fault for going to the party when he told her not to. Oh! And that henbane was the only way to deal with a clucking hen of a girlfriend."

"Would you be able to recognize the man if you saw him again?"

"I'm pretty sure," Mark nodded. "It was dark, but not that dark. The pathways are well lit."

"How much henbane would it take to knock out a nymph?" I asked Anya.

"A considerable amount," she told me after

thinking about it. "We generally don't use henbane for sleep or pain because it requires so much of it to work on us. It would taste horrible. Practically half the cup would have to be the herb to make a dent in us."

Fortuna gasped. "Could this all have been some horrible accident because Dergal was too drunk to drop off Ringmaster Phil's cup first and he got things mixed up?"

I stared at the seeress stunned. Could this have all been due to one person's drunken stupidity?

"I don't follow," Anya said as she squinted at Fortuna.

"What if Dergal got the drink from Jeannie, walked toward Uncle Phil's tent but got sidetracked when he saw Alessandra where he told her not to be," I hypothesized. "He spikes the drink and tries to force her to drink it so she'll stay asleep for the night, and he can do whatever it was he wanted to do. Mark then interferes. In his drunken state, he takes *that* spiked cup and leaves it on Uncle Phil's nightstand?"

"That doesn't explain someone trying to poison you earlier today, however," Fortuna pointed out.

"Humph. No, it doesn't," I agreed. "Mark,

would you mind going with us to make sure Dergal is the person you saw doing all this?"

"Sure, ring—Charlotte. I'm happy to help in any way I can.

"I'm going to let you two handle this. I still haven't found my sister. I want to go check a few places she might be," Anya said as she got up.

Once at the door, she turned toward Mark Botsworth. "You have my gratitude for helping my sister, human. If you ever need to call on me for aid, I will be there. I owe you a debt, and I mean to repay it." The warrior woman bowed, clicked her combat boots together as she rose, and left.

"I don't know whether to be honored or scared," Mark said once Anya was gone.

"Both is probably an appropriate reaction," I told him as I got up. He nodded, smiled, and then glanced worriedly toward the door.

CHAPTER 11

MARK, FORTUNA AND I STEPPED OUT OF HIS TENT and walked toward the backyard. My uncle had once explained the magic of the yurts kept there, but it still amazed me.

There were only six yurts behind the carousel to house more than a hundred paranormals, and one of those belonged only to the ringmaster. It didn't seem physically possible there were enough living quarters for everyone, yet my uncle insisted that the remainder of the inhabitants lived in the other five yurts.

"Each quarter is assigned to a group, and I help them arrange the interior. You know, so it suits their group," my uncle once explained. "The physical size of the yurt or the quarter assigned is of no consequence to what we can do inside."

"Kind of like a TARDIS?" I asked him. My *Dr. Who* reference went right over his ringmaster top hat.

I had never felt comfortable asking to be invited inside anyone else's living quarters, so I had seen none of the quarters that housed many people.

Honestly, I had asked no one because I didn't want to seem like a complete idiot. I mean, it was my family circus. As a younger teen, I wanted no one to know that I didn't know what they looked like.

Once I got older, it was just embarrassing.

"I believe this is the centaur quarters," Fortuna said as we came upon a yurt just south of my uncle's.

"Do we knock?" I asked. Fortuna raised her eyebrow. "Everyone always visited me in my quarters. Fiona said my room was much more private. I've never been in anyone's quarters other than mine and my uncle's."

"Well, you are in for a treat, then," Fortuna said as she held open the canvas.

While I had seen my uncle's room and it's incomprehensible size, and the kelpies row of rooms within their own tent, nothing could have prepared me for what the centaurs did with their living area.

Though there were only six centaurs at the Magical Midway, the interior was enormous. It didn't even look as if we were inside anything. The sky twinkled as if the ceiling was the image of a clear night in the desert, and a warm wind blew. The center was an expansive dirt road lined with three log cabins on either side.

"How is this even *here?*" I asked, stunned. "I mean, are we here? Or did we just go somewhere else?"

"We are definitely here," Fortuna laughed. "This will go with us wherever we move to. And it's here because of your magic, Charlotte."

The seer is correct, Samson told me. *When needed, your uncle or I will help you learn to change these interiors. Most groups have things the way they wish them to be, so you are unlikely to need to create an interior entirely.*

"Wow," I breathed as I gaped at the intricate centaur living space. I gazed down toward the end of the dirt road and saw a small seventh building with bars on the windows. "Is that, like, a centaur jail?"

"It is the containment room," Ningul said as

he and Fiona came in behind us. "We don't like to call it jail. It is used to hold a centaur safely until he can sober up."

"He *or* she," a female centaur called as she came out of the first house on the left side of the street. "Let's not be sexist when it comes to which centaurs can and can't hold their liquor, Ningul."

"Ringmaster, this is Femeg," Ningul introduced her as she walked up to us.

"Please, just call me Meg. Nice to meet you," she said as she stuck out her hand. I nodded and shook it. "I have to tell you, I'm really excited that there's a female ringmaster. I've never been around for a female ringmaster."

"Please, call me Charlotte," I told her. I wondered if it wouldn't be easier just to tattoo *Call Me Charlotte* across my forehead. It was a phrase I seemed to repeat on an hourly basis.

"How is Dergal doing?" Ningul asked Meg.

"I visited him about an hour ago," she told him as we all ambled toward the containment cabin. "Once he sobered up his attitude went down at least a few notches. Not enough to completely alleviate his sexist pigdom, but enough that we were able to have a normal conversation with an epithet every other sentence instead of every sentence."

"Were you able to get any answers out of him?"

"A few," Meg told him as we continued walking toward the building. "He was the one that put henbane in the ringmasters' drink today. He said his intention was simply to, and I quote, 'get that witch off my case for a while.' He didn't seem to understand the gravity of the situation."

"He never does."

"He also didn't realize that too much henbane could disconnect a witch from their body," she added. "Once I informed him of that fundamental magical fact, he turned as pale as a ghost."

We walked up to the small, barred cabin and Ningul climbed the small step to enter a code in a very fancy electronic system on the old wooden door. As he swung the door open, he turned to Meg. "There's no one in here."

"That's impossible, I checked on him just an hour ago. He was right here!" The five of us scrambled into the tiny cabin to check it for ourselves. As we jostled and pushed against one another, we each confirmed that the cabin was empty and Dergal was gone.

"Who knows the code?" I asked Ningul.

"Well, all the centaurs know the code," Ningul said as he continued looking around the cabin as if willing himself to find Dergal tucked in a darkened corner. "This is not a jail, Charlotte. This is simply a way for us to contain a centaur that may be in the grips of temporary madness. All of us have the code, and the ability to place someone here."

"The person contained cannot reach the keypad to enter the code, so there is no reason to keep the code secret," Meg said. Ningul and Meg seemed to be so sure of themselves that I could not believe one of them hadn't thought of the loophole glaring them in the face.

"But the person inside could tell someone else the code to let them out," I pointed out to them both as kindly and patiently as I could. Ningul shook his head.

"But who would let them out?"

"Well, who can come in your quarters? Are they magically protected in any way?"

"Of course not, we're centaurs. We can stomp on anyone. We also like to throw parties in our quarters a lot," Meg said. "All our individual houses lock so there never seemed to be a reason to do anything like that."

"So anyone could've walked in here, talked to Dergal through the bars, got the code, and let him out."

"Well," Ningul said slowly. "I suppose it's possible—"

"Alessandra," Fortuna interrupted. "No man could pass the waterfall, so she had to have left her area on her own. Anya said she keeps returning to him. It's the *only* logical explanation; no one else would have let him out."

"We need to find them," I said, turning toward the entrance. "With the protection I put on Dergal, he can't physically hurt her, but if Anya finds them together, he can't defend himself, either."

"Do we really care?" Mark asked quietly as the group turned to stare at him. I stopped in mid-stride and turned back toward the group. While each face appeared slightly troubled, every expression seemed hesitant to disagree.

"I care," I told them. "Despite never having wanted this job, it is mine now. And I'm not about to let vigilante justice rain down on any member of the Magical Midway. That's not justice. That's revenge. And it's not right."

"Of course, Ringmaster," Mark said, and then sighed. "It's hard not to want revenge against someone that I watched hurt someone else without any regret or concern. Especially someone as sweet and lovely as Alessandra."

Oh, my goodness. Spring has sprung, and love is in the air. The moon has only risen twice on my reign as ringmaster, and this place is already a soap opera. "I understand, Mark," I told him as I turned back toward the exit. "No offense taken, let's just find them."

The party for my ascension was in full swing under the Big Top when we all arrived. I scanned the crowd for Dergal or Alessandra, but I didn't see either of them.

"Ringmaster!" Wendy Marmontel called as she clutched my hand. I had known the sylph since I was a young girl and remembered her fondly for the balloon animals she always made for me. The fact that her long hair always had every appearance of blowing in a breeze that seemed to follow her, though, still freaked me out a little. "So glad to see you have finally joined us! Please accept my condolences for the loss of your uncle, and let him know that I say hi the next time you see him."

"Of course. Have you seen Alessandra or Dergal by chance?"

"No, I do my best to *avoid* Dergal. If I do see

him, I make sure the wind blows him just a few feet away from me," Wendy smiled. "The wind is always happy to oblige. Alessandra, though, lovely girl. I could swear I saw her near the small diving pool earlier."

"Thanks," I nodded and continued to make my way through the crowd. "And please, call me Charlotte."

Look up, Samson said sharply. As I raised my eyes, I pinpointed Dergal standing on the eastern tightrope platform just above the small diving pool used for shows. My eyes followed the taut rope stretched across the Big Top, and I spotted Alessandra seated on the western platform. She casually dangled her legs in the air as she stared at her abusive love.

Oh, my gosh, what the heck is this? I asked Samson.

Drama? Samson replied. *The safety net has been taken down.*

We have a safety net? We don't have magic to keep people from falling?"

No, Samson replied. *We used to until we lost The Flying Pandas in '36. Their own magic interfered with the safety net magic, and they all went splat during a practice.*

Oh my gosh. That's terrible!

In any case, there is no safety net, Samson repeated.

The pair were so high up that I couldn't hear what they were saying to one another. *Is there any way to make it so I can listen to what they're saying?*

Yes, Uncle Phil broke into the discussion. I watched him float brightly up to the pair. Though he could get close to them, he could do nothing in his ephemeral state. *Think of their names and then broadcast. The entire Big Top will be able to hear what they're saying. Perhaps exposing what's going on up there will stop it.*

Uncle Phil, they're doing this in the middle of the Big Top in the middle of a party the entire Midway is attending. That's not going to stop it.

I would suggest you at least try, he said.

I closed my eyes and took a deep breath. *Dergal, Alessandra, broadcast.*

"—and if you had just stayed home from the party like I told you to, none of this would've happened!" Dergal's angry voice screeched through the enormous red and white striped tent. The chattering din of happy partygoers suddenly fell silent as they turned to each other in confusion.

"Did you give the cup of henbane to the ringmaster?" Alessandra asked in her soft voice.

Her whispered tone echoed as if through speakers. The party attendees were pointing above their heads as they slowly realized what was going on.

"I don't have to stand here and answer your questions," Dergal snapped and reached for the rung to climb down. Water from the diving pool shot forcefully against his hand causing him to release his grip. "Let me down from here!"

Dergal was sopping wet from head to toe, and I understood precisely how Alessandra had managed to get him up on the platform. She hadn't broken Dergal out because, as Anya feared, she was still in love with him and wanted him back. She had broken him out of the containment cabin because there had been no water nearby that she could use to control him.

"You tried to drug me," Alessandra said quietly. "You tried to make me drink the cup that you held in your hand. Did you then bring that cup full of henbane to our ringmaster's tent? Did you kill our ringmaster?"

"You're crazy," Dergal spat at her. "You're a crazy woman. Stupid nymph. I didn't kill *anyone*. And none of it would've happened, anyway, if you had just done what I told you and stayed home!"

He was mean *and* dumb, apparently.

The crowd assembled below gasped in horror as Dergal unintentionally admitted his role in Uncle Phil's death without realizing that he was doing so. Dergal's eyes grew round as saucers as he took in the expressions of shock, horror, and anger in the crowd beneath him. His head snapped up and his face twisted with rage.

"Look at what you've done!" the angry centaur shouted at Alessandra. His eyes scanned over the crowd and found me as I stared up at him. "And you! How dare you broadcast our words! If your father had been chosen ringmaster, he wouldn't have done such a thing! You never should have been chosen!"

"I never *would've* been chosen if you hadn't killed my uncle, you moron!" I shouted angrily back at him. Despite my voice not being broadcast like Alessandra and Dergal's, the Big Top was so quiet that every paranormal in the place could hear me. The crowd murmured in agreement. "It was your own actions that caused this tragic cascade of events that you are so unhappy with."

"It wasn't my actions! It was her! It was her! If she had just done what I told her, none of this would've happened!" Dergal screamed hysterically.

"Are you so sure?" Alessandra asked calmly as she pulled her legs back in and stood up. "Are you, Dergal? Are you willing to bet your life on the fact that none of this was your fault, and all of it was mine?"

This is not good, Samson said.

What's happening? I asked him.

Alessandra is about to give him the Siren's Call, Samson said. *If he's wrong, he'll drown. If he's right, he'll survive. He's not right, though. We all know he's about as wrong as someone can be. He does not realize that, though. If I had to place bets, that boy is about to become a flotation device.*

"Of course I'm right," he shouted at her as he gripped the platform pole with his fists. "What have I been trying to tell you all this time? I'm right, you're wrong. You just don't know your place."

Oh, man, this guy was getting under my skin.

Uncle Phil, what are my choices here? I thought to him.

He is guilty of manslaughter, so what I would do his hand him over to the Witches' Council, Uncle Phil said. *However, I must point out Alessandra is giving him a choice to bet his life. He doesn't have to, and she is not forcing him to do so. If he does, in my mind, that's his own choice to make.*

The entire Big Top held its breath waiting for someone to say something. In that suspended moment, I had to make a choice. A step toward what type of ringmaster I wanted to be. Was I the type of ringmaster that would protect them from even their own terrible decisions? Or would I let people fall on their face and accept the consequences they asked for?

"Would you bet your life on it, Dergal?" Alessandra asked again.

I thought about what Uncle Phil said, how his father had demanded that he do things his way which robbed him of the ability to learn. In the end, it was Uncle Phil's choice to let me trip and fall a little bit, to feel my way through that decided it for me.

"Dergal, do you need my help?" I called to him. "I can stop this if what is happening is not something you consent to. You have only to ask."

I felt someone squeeze my arm and glanced to my right to find Anya standing beside me looking up at her sister proudly.

Dergal stood straight and glowered down at me.

"Hell no, I don't need *your* help. I would bet my life on the fact that I am right and you are wrong. Especially *you*," he spat with as much disgust as he could muster as he shoved his finger in my direction.

Alessandra extended her arms and glowed as her lips parted. The most beautiful note I have ever heard flowed from her. A white haze raced like an ocean wave from her to Dergal.

As it gathered around him, his eyes snapped open, and his face turned white. The nymph's note hit a crescendo, and Dergal tumbled forward off the platform to the gasps of the gathered crowd.

He landed with a splash in the tiny diving pool below.

The energy of the Magical Midway felt lighter as I opened my eyes to the bright morning. My second conscious day as the carnival's ringmaster was the first one I looked forward to.

"Flag's up, lazybones! You can actually eat Hildegaard's French toast this morning!" Fiona said as she breezed in.

"Do you have some kind of psychic awareness of when a witch wakes up? I swear, I've barely opened my eyes, and you're bouncing into my tent," I asked her as I pulled the covers back over my head to block out the light and her cheerfulness.

"It's not my fault you don't zip your door closed when you go to sleep. That, and you groan every morning when you wake up," Fiona told me as she flopped down on a chair next to my bed. "You groan *loudly*. I suspect the lares at the security station can hear you when you wake up. And they *must* know when you groan that you're waking, or they would rush in here to see who was killing you."

"How are you this cheerful before your coffee?" I asked as I threw the covers off and scooted toward the edge of the bed.

"I love life, your highness."

"Stop calling me that," I told her as I brushed my hair. "You're cheerful because you spent the night consoling Ningul."

"I don't know what you're talking about," Fiona scoffed while blushing.

"That's okay. I know what I'm talking about. How's he doing, by the way? Even if he didn't like Dergal, I can't believe what happened last night didn't bother him a bit."

"I think he was bothered by the fact that he didn't see it was getting as bad as it was. He feels terribly guilty that one of his own centaurs was responsible for your Uncle Phil's death."

He shouldn't, Uncle Phil said as he shimmered into view. *I think many of us overlooked Dergal's behavior far more than we should have. Myself included. Morning, girls.*

"Morning, Uncle Phil," I told him. "Hey, Fiona, can you grab me some coffee from Hildegaard's? I need to talk to my uncle."

"You just don't want to change out of your pajamas," Fiona teased as she hopped up. "Peppermint Pride?"

"How about Caramel Competence this morning?" Fiona rolled her eyes. "What?"

"I'll pretend it's for me. I am not going into the food tent and telling anyone that I'm getting Caramel Competence for the ringmaster. People have been freaked out enough as it is," she said as she walked out.

So how are you this morning? Uncle Phil asked.

"I'm...I don't know how I am," I told him as I sat back down on the bed. "Somebody died last night, Uncle Phil. And I *let* it happen. I know what I thought when I let Dergal make a choice to refuse my help. But I can't shake the fact that I stood by and let it happen."

You did, Uncle Phil agreed. *The fact that you're questioning yourself and whether you should have is a good sign, Charlotte. I'd be more concerned if you woke up this morning and didn't have second thoughts.*

"Was what I did right?"

I can't answer that. Only you can answer that.

Paranormal deaths at the Midway were strange affairs. Paranormals knew that death was not the end but only a transition to another realm.

When people grieved, they grieved for what they lost when the deceased disappeared from their life. They did not, though, grieve for what the dead lost. No one felt sorry for someone who died. They knew that person was all right.

Jeannie mourned Uncle Phil because she had lost him. The Magical Midway mourned Uncle Phil because they lost a leader. No one worried about Uncle Phil now, they only missed him because he was no longer here with them.

At least not that they could see, anyway.

Dergal's death was not one that anyone in the Midway wept over. He was not liked by anyone, at least as far as I could tell. No one missed him, and as morning dawned, no one cared that he was gone. The assembled paranormals had even been somewhat annoyed that I called a halt to the party after his death.

That no one mourned Dergal, that he lived a life so unremarkable that no one missed him was sad. That many on the Midway today were relieved that he was gone was even more tragic.

"I let him make a choice," I said finally to Uncle Phil. "I think that was right. I think it was better than making a choice for him."

Well, then it was right, Uncle Phil smiled. Gee, thanks, Uncle Phil. What the heck is the point of a guide if he just agrees with everything you do?

"I do have a question. Where did his body go?"

Ah, yes, our special sparkle death, Uncle Phil laughed. *I will admit that I didn't say anything to you, just so I could see the look on your face when you went over to the pool.*

"Um, thanks? Very funny."

There is an enchantment within the magic that turns anyone who has died into sparkle ash.

"You mean glitter?"

No, I mean sparkle ash, Uncle Phil repeated. *As soon as someone has passed on, their body combusts so quickly that no human eye can see it. What is left is a pile of sparkle ash. That sparkle ash can be given back to loved ones if the deceased has a family in one of the paranormal towns and expanded back into a body, or interred like any other cremated remains.*

"What happens if someone's killed?"

Well, they turn into sparkle ash. We wouldn't want any of the humans coming across a dead body in their wanderings through the carnival or circus, would we?

"But how do you gather evidence? I mean, if someone's turned into sparkle ash all the evidence of how they died and who killed them gets combusted into glitter bits," I pointed out to Uncle Phil.

Yes, true, I never thought about that. How often would that happen, really? Murders at the Midway? Honestly, Charlotte, I don't think it's anything for you to worry about, Uncle Phil said.

"Yeah, you're probably right," I agreed with him.

CHAPTER 12

As the week ended, the carnival seemed to settle back into normalcy. The inhabitants of the Magical Midway even appeared slightly more confident in my ability to lead them, if the cheerful greetings were any indication.

Slightly.

I finally made the rounds, stopping to visit all the paranormal groups that called this traveling patch of existence home. It was a remarkably motley crew of strange creatures. Most seemed friendly, some seemed suspicious of me, and some were suspiciously cagey as all get out.

"We *are* still a traveling carnival," Fiona told me late that afternoon as we sat in the communications area sipping Flukum Slush, an icy grape drink that Hildegaard whipped up on hot days. "You've heard of the carnie code, right?"

"No," I shook my head. "What's that?"

"To put it simply, it's us against the world. In the carnie world, locals are to be held at arm's length. We're always a little suspicious of them— that's true in human carnivals, by the way. Add to the fact that we're the paranormal carnival, and we're doubly suspicious."

"That doesn't seem to make for a very friendly carnival," I told her, frowning.

"It's all an act, Charlotte. Everything in every carnival is an act. While we want to make them happy, we do it to take the money, yeah? So, they are suspicious of us because we'll only be there a few days and then we disappear. We're suspicious of them because they are not us, and there are many things we don't want them to find out."

"This place always seem so magical and perfect to me. You're making it sound kind of… well, sleazy and cagey."

"No, it isn't really. But we do walk a middle path. The middle way, ya ken? Midway? Middle way? The people in the paranormal towns just keep the humans out. Problem solved. Humans couldn't see the towns if they were staring right at them. We mix with humans regularly and even use our magic to put on a show for them. That's risky."

"Then why does everybody do it? I mean, what's the point of living in fear?" Fiona blew her long hair off her face with a loud exhalation of breath and rested her chin on her hand. "What? I don't get it."

"We're rebels. We don't live like everyone else. We're not who the humans expect us to be. We don't do what the paranormals expect us to do. We're outsiders. But we *like* being outsiders," Fiona explained. "Besides, where else can we all get a custom house for free because the ringmaster blinks it into existence?"

"I can understand that part of it, at least," I admitted as I gave the once-over to Uncle Phil's man cave of a sitting area. "Speaking of which, I think it's time to redecorate. We solved Uncle Phil's death, Dergal decided to deal with himself. I think I want something a little less masculine."

"Well, you can do it with the blink of an eye," Fiona said. She stood up and walked around the cauldron cave considering what she thought I should do. "Can we get Netflix?"

"Do we even have Internet?"

"Well, no. But you could do that, couldn't you?"

Knowledge must be earned, not magicked, Samson said as he walked in.

"I don't feel like being able to watch cats on YouTube because I magicked an Internet connection is really cheating, Samson," I told my familiar as he jumped up on the cauldron.

I do, he answered. *You must call your parents. You haven't spoken to your mother since dinner last night, and since you didn't call for breakfast or lunch, they are both frantic.*

"Oh, shoot," I jumped up out of the chair. "Wait, how do you know that?"

Your father's ability to speak to anything alive can travel remarkable distances when he is intentionally shouting in said creature's direction, Samson told me. *My heightened familiar senses likely enabled him to reach me faintly, but he is definitely yelling.*

I ran over to the cauldron and asked to call my father. The steam and bubbles whooshed upwards as my panic-stricken father slowly solidified.

"My goodness, Charlotte, are you all right? Your mother and I have been worried sick about you!"

"I'm really sorry, Dad," I told him as I reached toward him. "Things got really, really crazy last night. The good news is we figured out what happened to Uncle Phil. It turns out it was all an accident."

"An accident? How on earth could he be killed by accident?"

I spent the next half-hour explaining to my father the ins and outs of the past couple of days. As I was telling him what happened, I realized just how much of the investigation and discovering Dergal's issues, and actions had rested upon me.

"Today has been the first day where everything is kind of normal and somewhat calmed down. Again, I'm really sorry for not calling last night and worrying you guys when I didn't call for breakfast."

"I understand, Charlotte," Dad said. "Your mother, on the other hand…"

"I know, I know."

My father turned and spoke away from me so I couldn't hear the conversation between him and my mom. After a minute or two, he turned back. "Your mother would like me to relay to you that she would like us to come to visit today."

"Okay, give me some time to figure out where we are and where the closest airport is and—" My father held up his hand, and I waited.

Quite a while.

"Your mother has asked me to tell you that she is well aware that you are a near omnipotent witch with superpowers as well as sitting in a traveling town that houses many creatures with superpowers and that you surely can find a way to get us there without the use of an airplane." Dad turned to her again and nodded, holding his hands up in defeat. "She asked if there were any genies at the Magical Midway?"

"Yes, Uncle Phil's girlfriend, in fact."

"Your mother wants you to go and ask the genie to grant your wish to bring both of us to the Magical Midway," Dad said. "Once we're there, your magic can send us home."

"Will that work?" I asked Samson.

If Jeannie will grant you the wish, Samson replied.

"Okay, I'm on it," I told Dad. "Do you want me to call you again before I make the wish so you guys will be ready?"

"Your mother informs me I will be ready immediately, so no," Dad smiled weakly. "We'll see you soon."

"Hopefully," I told Dad. "I'll go see Jeannie now."

We disconnected from the cauldron call, and I

started the short walk toward Jeannie's Snack Shop.

Jeannie's building was no longer dark, but her windows were still snapped shut. "I bet Uncle Phil's in there with her," I said quietly to Fiona as we walked around the back to knock on the door.

"Probably," Fiona responded. "They were quite close when he was alive. I was actually surprised that they didn't marry before...well, before your uncle died."

"Really? They didn't even share a yurt, though."

"Djinn don't sleep," Fiona told me as she rapped on the closed wooden door. "Jeannie doesn't actually have living quarters because she doesn't need a sleeping area. You can almost always find her here at the shop, or at your Uncle Phil's place. Well, you used to."

The door cracked open, and the older woman smiled at me with a hesitant friendliness. "Hello, Charlotte. It's so nice of you and Fiona to stop by to check on me. I'm so sorry about the other day."

"Please, don't apologize," I told her as she opened the door wider for Fiona and me to slip through. "It can't be easy to lose someone that way."

"No, it's definitely not," Jeannie told me as we closed the door behind us. I immediately noticed the shimmery glow across the room.

Hello, girls, Uncle Phil called from his seat on the counter.

"Hey, wait a minute—" Fiona said as she pointed. "Can't you...you know...I mean, you did for me, right? Why not?"

"Actually, I can do better than that, can't I?" I realized that not only could I make it so Jeannie could hear Uncle Phil, but that she could see him, too. I met Uncle Phil's eyes and held my hands up in a silent question, not wanting to clue Jeannie into what we were discussing if there was a reason he didn't want me to make him...well, alive to her again.

That's an exciting proposition, my girl, Uncle Phil said as he tapped his finger against his chin. *I don't know why I didn't think of it. Not perfect, but adequate. Clearly, I can't be all that I was to her. My uncle wiggled the facsimile of his eyebrows. If you get my meaning.*

"Oh, man, please, let's pretend I didn't," I shuddered as I glanced back and forth from the round older woman to my fat uncle. "I didn't need that image in my head. Really."

"I feel like I'm missing something," Jeannie said as she glanced at me in confusion. "Did I forget to clean up something?" She looked around at the spotless building.

"No, no, Jeannie. I was…" I paused, trying to think through the ramifications of letting Jeannie know that Uncle Phil was seated just two feet to her right. I didn't want to hurt the woman, but it seemed unfair to keep the information from her.

And, frankly, it seemed like half the Midway knew that he was still here, anyway. I was somewhat surprised that she didn't realize I was still talking to him. "I was talking to Uncle Phil's ghost."

"He's here?" she asked, bursting into tears. "Here, in this very room, right now?"

"Yep. In fact, he's been in this room with you so much that he hasn't been spending all that much time with me teaching me what I need to know. Just sayin'." I shot Uncle Phil a look. "I can enable you to hear him and see him. Would you like me to do that?"

"Permanently?"

"I *think* so." I looked at Uncle Phil, and he nodded. "Yes, I could do that."

"Oh, please, Charlotte," Jeannie wept as she raced across the room and clutched my hands. "I miss him so very much. I've been so lonely without him."

If I could do this for Jeannie, was there even a point to keeping Uncle Phil an invisible ghost? The ghosts inside the Haunted House could be seen by anyone, including humans that visited the attraction. Someone must have enabled that years ago. Is there any reason I shouldn't make Uncle Phil visible? To everyone?

Your uncle was the ringmaster, Samson reminded me. *Having two ringmasters walking around could get confusing. There also could be unforeseen consequences. It's never been done.*

It would not be that big of a deal, I told him. *He won't be plugged back into the ringmaster power or anything, right?*

Power is more than just magic, Charlotte.

I want everyone that's connected magically to the Magical Midway able to see and hear Uncle Phil, I thought after closing my eyes. Upon opening them, I found all three staring at me. "Did it work?" I asked.

Uncle Phil hopped down from the counter and slowly put his sparkly hand in front of Jeannie's gaze. Her eyes widened as she stared down at the ghostly palm hovering in front of her nose. Turning, the shocked djinn looked up at Uncle Phil and smiled. "You're pink!" she laughed.

"And blue! Let's not forget the blue," he smiled. "I've missed our talks. I wish I could hug you, my Jeannie."

"Granted!" Jeannie shouted and clapped her hands.

Uh oh.

The shimmering sparkles around the ghostly outline of Uncle Phil grew bright and brighter still. With a loud crack that hurt my ears, the lights disappeared, and Uncle Phil stood in the snack shack looking for all the world like he had never died. Jeannie threw herself into his arms. Though my uncle embraced her back, he caught my eye.

I'm not sure this was a good idea, Uncle Phil sent. *Can't I just undo it?*

You can't undo a granted wish, Uncle Phil responded. *You can make me invisible again, but I'll still have...whatever this mass is. Unless I wish for it to go away and she grants it. I don't even know how that would work. And I don't know if she will.*

I tried to warn you, Samson pointed out.

~

I took about ten minutes of walking around the
Midway with Uncle Phil's reconstituted ghost to
realize that I had just made my ringmaster
ascension a million times harder than it had been.
Maybe. The word of his pseudo-resurrection
spread like wildfire, and supernaturals came from
all corners of the grounds to see him again.

"You didn't think that one through, did you?"
Fortuna asked as she wiggled her way out of the
crowd pressed against the former ringmaster and
walked over to Fiona and me on the edge of the
near-riot. "Everyone's asking him questions
about when we'll open, where we're going next."

"Questions they never bothered to ask me. I
know."

"They *know* him. Knew him as ringmaster for
years," Fiona said as she watched the thrall of
excitement. "People don't like change. They like
what's familiar. He's familiar."

"Fantastic."

"Look, this could be a good thing," Fortuna
said quietly. "You really weren't trained at all, and
you haven't spent much time here. Your uncle
could take some of the pressure off you since he
can step in with the more mundane, operational
aspects. It might not be a bad thing."

"He's a man," Fiona scoffed. "Now that he has

a body and everyone can hear him, he'll be acting like he's back in charge in no time."

The three of us watched as Uncle Phil shook hands and hugged friend after friend. Fortuna was right, and Fiona was right. I likely just made it much more difficult for the people of Magical Midway to see me as the ringmaster, but I also just bought myself some time to learn while having a safety net.

As far as trade-offs go, it seemed fair.

There was also the simple fact that Uncle Phil was murdered. No ringmaster had ever been killed before him, and he was robbed of time he shouldn't have been. My father's brother didn't get to marry or have children. He lost so much, and watching Jeannie happily cling to Uncle Phil's hip as everyone welcomed him back made me feel like this was the right thing to do.

Even if it made my journey a little bumpier.

"I'm all right with it," I told them both. "This was never going to be easy for me, anyway."

"I've been raised to take over the Makepeace Circus since I was a little boy," Gunther Makepeace said as he joined our conversation. "Personally, I think I might have preferred the way you came to the job. Must be nice to just make some things up as you go."

"Gunther!" I jumped. "What are you doing here?"

"My father got a call that Phil Astley had come back from the dead. He asked me to 'sneak in and spy' to find out what was going on. So, I walked in and decided just to ask you," Gunther smiled. He swung his eyes toward Uncle Phil and ticked his chin in the crowd's direction. "That's something we haven't seen before."

As we stood at the edge, I explained to Gunther the series of events that resulted in Uncle Phil standing at the center of the clearing and holding court with the residents of the Magical Midway. "So, he's not alive, really. He just…looks and sounds alive."

"Fascinating," Gunther murmured.

"Why would your Dad even care? And how on earth did he find out so fast? I mean, this literally happened less than an hour ago."

"The Makepeace spies, Charlotte," Fiona said.

"Spies?" I blinked. Fiona rolled her eyes at me.

"The fairs are protected from remote viewing for some reason," Gunther explained. "So, if you want to know what's going on within them, you have to send someone to join, and they report back to whoever sent them. We have a few in our number, too."

"We have spies at your circus?"

"You do. Two that I know of."

"Why would we send spies? Heck, why would anyone send spies to a circus?"

"Witches are nosy," Gunther laughed. "It drives the Witches' Council crazy that they can't just wave their wands and take a peek at what either of us is doing. They can look into the human world, any paranormal town. But they can't just peek in on us, or on you."

"Witches don't have wands. That's just human fairy tales."

Gunther reached into his back pocket and pulled out a white wood drumstick, or so I thought. He held it up in front of him, squinted his eyes, and the stick glowed. The excited throng gathered around Uncle Phil grew silent as they all stopped to stare warily at Gunther.

"I stand corrected," I told him as I stared at the thin stick thrumming with power. "Now put that away before you freak everybody out even more."

"Where did you go to school? I can't believe you were never taught wand work. That's pretty basic stuff," he asked as he slipped the wand back into his pocket.

"Mickwac, Texas."

Gunther frowned. "I don't recall any Witches' Academies there."

"I went to human school." His eyes grew wide, and one eyebrow raised. "What? Haven't you ever met a witch that went to human school before?"

"Honestly? No." Gunther shrugged.

"Our Charlotte was raised by my brother," Uncle Phil boomed after he extracted himself from his admirers and reached out his newly formed hand to shake Gunther's. "My brother never met a witch lesson he didn't want to keep her from. Hello, young Gunther. Your father got you here in record time, I see."

"Mr. Astley," Gunther nodded respectfully. "It's delightful to see you again. Especially since I didn't expect to ever see you again."

"Are you staying for dinner? I found out I can eat!" Uncle Phil told him excitedly. Jeannie giggled and squeezed him. "But I don't *have* to eat, which is a nice talent I plan to never, ever take advantage of. Makes me feel better about losing all of my other talents."

"Well, not *all* your talents," Jeannie interjected and blushed. Then she giggled like a schoolgirl.

Oh, gross.

"Uncle Phil, if I don't get Mom and Dad here, I

think my Mom might slap me silly. It's been over an hour."

"Of course! Let's go into my yurt where we can bring them in a bit more privately."

His yurt. When I woke up this morning it was *my* yurt. Now it's his yurt. What's a ringmaster without a yurt of her own?

A homeless ringmaster? Samson asked.

Charlotte, my apologies, Uncle Phil thought toward me as his eyebrows lowered.

We can still talk telepathically?

Of course, I am still a ghost. No matter what Jeannie attached to my spirit to make it look like it is encased in a body, I am still a ghost. After your parents leave, you and I can talk about how we move forward like this. Or how to undo it, if you prefer.

I frowned but nodded.

"So, young Gunther, will you join us?" Uncle Phil asked again.

"Well, Dad does expect a full reconnaissance mission, with all the sneaking around and turning over stones that would normally entail. I imagine that would take a while, so sure," he smiled.

Wow, he was handsome. His teeth were so perfectly white and straight they practically glowed against his tan face.

"Thank you for the invitation," Gunther said as he gazed at me. I smiled.

"Of course," Uncle Phil waved off his thanks and turned toward the private yurt. "After all, you and Charlotte are the future of the paranormal circuses. You should get to know one another, I should think."

"I'd like that very much. She's fascinating," Gunther answered as his soft, sea-green eyes fell on me. I blushed. "I mean, it's not often you meet a witch that doesn't know the first thing about being one."

Well, that warm, fuzzy feeling didn't last long.

CHAPTER 13

UNCLE PHIL, JEANNIE, FIONA, FORTUNA, Gunther, and I piled into Uncle Phil's yurt condo and sat around a dining table I could *swear* was way smaller this morning. My uncle had motioned for me to take the head seat at the table, and I did. Gunther quickly moved to take the position next to me.

"Make the wish, dear girl," Uncle Phil told me. I nodded and wished for my parents to join us here at the Magical Midway. As soon as the words left my lips, Jeannie shouted that my wish was granted and my parents instantly appeared standing next to the table as if they had just blinked into existence.

Djinn magic was useful, but witch magic was way prettier.

"Oh my gosh!" my father shouted as he grasped the back of the chair in front of him to steady himself as he stared at my smiling uncle. "You're not dead! How are you not dead?"

"I am dead. I am *quite* dead, in fact."

While my father stared at his brother in shock, I frantically explained how Uncle Phil's lifelike appearance had come to pass.

"I can't sense you or speak to you," my father said in confusion.

"Well, no, you can't. I'm *dead*. Your talent only works on things that live. I thought we went over this already? Alan, you are just as stubborn as you always were, and you still don't listen."

My father stood up straight and took a deep breath. For a moment, I thought that another Astley throw-down was imminent. It was only a moment, though. Seconds passed, and my father's expression softened.

As the two brothers stood in front of one another, my father reached out slowly and hugged my uncle tightly. It was a beautiful, touching moment, and I was grateful I had been a part of making it happen.

Until my mother wiped her eyes and turned

to look at me with that stormy expression that heralded another Astley throw-down imminently threatening.

"Charlotte Esmeralda Astley! I could throttle you!"

"Your middle name is Esmeralda? That's kinda witchy," Fiona whispered to the left of me. I kicked her under the table and braced for my mother's lecture.

"Your father and I were terrified that something had happened to you! How could you call and tell us that someone was trying to kill you and then *not* call when mealtime came? I stood in my kitchen for two hours holding scrambled eggs and waiting for you!" she hollered as she shook her finger in my face. "That was very irresponsible of you! Your father and I were worried sick, and we had no way to contact you!"

"I'm sorry, Mom, I really am," I told her as I did my best to look remorseful and as guilty as I knew she wanted me to feel. "You are absolutely right, I didn't stop and think what you and Dad would go through not hearing from me. Entirely my fault, and I won't do it again."

"I should say *not*," my mother harrumphed, crossing her arms. "Well, at least your uncle is back, and you can come home now."

"Martha, I am not the ringmaster again," Uncle Phil told her as her face fell. "While I can help Charlotte out a little more than before since everyone can see and hear me, the power's anchored in her. She cannot leave for any length of time. She is *still* the ringmaster."

"Mom, I promise I'll try not to worry you. I have a lot of people here working to protect me." Granted, they seem to have no idea how to investigate, and they overlooked things happening right under their noses, but they meant well. Mostly.

"You wouldn't have to depend on others if you learned to magic," Gunther pointed out. All heads around the table snapped to stare at Roland Makepeace's son, and he shifted uneasily in his chair.

"What do you mean?" I asked him.

"I'm sorry, I don't mean to interrupt or interject myself into a family discussion. I do, however, have some experience in being trained to be an heir. It seems incredibly irresponsible for you to hold the position you do with absolutely no understanding of magic or an ability to use it."

Well, thanks for your input, Mr. Know-it-all. So glad that you're here to mansplain this all to me.

"I have an understanding of magic," I argued. "I've blinked like four times and made big things happen. I mean, clearly, I have a lot to learn, but as soon as I became the ringmaster, I got this super magic ability, and I've used it. So, you know...I'm fine. Really."

"That's not magic, Charlotte," Gunther told me. "Well, it is, but it's not *yours*. The power belongs to whatever animates the Midway. If it doesn't want you to do what you're asking it to do, it simply won't do it. You should have your own ability that you can count on, that you know will always work precisely the way you expect. And right now you really don't."

"Is this true?" I asked Uncle Phil.

"It is...it's not quite that simple, but on the whole, what Gunther said is correct," Uncle Phil agreed. "For example, if you wanted to kill Samson, you would not be allowed to do so."

Why would she want to kill me? I'm charming, Samson said.

"So, wait a minute...All these rules that you're telling me to apply to what I can and can't do. Those aren't magic rules? Those are just things that the Magical Midway's spirit thing will and won't let me do?"

"Some are rules. Some are rules that can be

changed. Some are immutable limitations," my uncle said.

"How do I know which is which, then?"

Silence.

"I swear, this is going to give me a headache. On a daily basis," I told the assembled group. "Uncle Phil, were you trained as a witch? Like, a regular witch."

"Years and years and years ago, Charlotte."

"Mom? Dad?"

"Charlotte, we remember some things from when we were children, but your father and I haven't used those skills much over the years because…" Mom's eyes flashed over toward my father, and she left the truth of what we both knew unsaid.

"Charlotte…" Dad said, but I jumped in to head him off. I could see my father's discomfort growing as we all spoke, and I didn't want to go down a rabbit-hole of regret. It just didn't matter anymore.

"Look, Dad, I get that you have some regrets and none of this is precisely the way you thought it would turn out. I'm not trying to make you feel bad. I am trying to understand who I am now, and what I need to know. I'm not trying to make you feel guilty. If you want to help me, help me figure out what my next step is."

The room fell silent. After a time, Gunther leaned over.

"Can I talk to you for a second?"

"You have another judgment you wish to pass on me?" I snapped as I sat up straighter in my chair. Gunther's face remained impassive as our eyes clashed, but he leaned forward and spoke as softly and gently as he could.

"I'm sorry if what I said hurt you, and no, I don't. But I would really like to talk to you. Alone," Gunther said as he passed his eyes over the assembled crowd listening intently to every word we said. "Can we take a walk?" Everyone appeared somewhat offended at Gunther's request.

I sense no malice or harmful intentions in him, Samson said. *Unfortunately, not the same can be said of his father. But young Gunther is probably not a chip off the old block. He does not mean to offend you.*

"Fine. You mind if Samson comes?" I asked him as I pushed out my chair.

"It wouldn't matter if I did," he laughed and pointed to the bulge in his chest. "Even when we think they left us alone, they don't leave us alone."

Gunther's hearty laugh deflated the sting of his words a little bit.

"We'll be back," I told everyone.

"Charlotte—"

"Dad, relax. Spend some time with Uncle Phil. I'll be fine."

Gunther and I walked silently toward the western clearing far away from the hustle and bustle of the carnival. While Uncle Phil and Roland Makepeace looked like they stepped out of a time long past, Gunther and I could have been any two modern humans visiting a park for the day. While walking their two cats.

Okay, maybe we looked a *little* odd.

"I know that you don't know me," Gunther began once there was a significant distance between us and everyone else. "Not only that, I'm the son of your current rival."

"Yeah, but are we *rivals*, really? We're both the same, sort of. Or will be. What do we even really have to do with one another? I feel like everybody turns this into high drama unnecessarily."

"I can guarantee you my father does not see it that way. When there were thirty or forty midways, individual families engaged in friendly rivalries. With just the two of us left, things have changed. The rivalry is not quite so friendly in his mind."

"This seems like more complication than is actually warranted in the situation. I'm just sayin'."

Gunther laughed, throwing his head back with a full smile that took over his face. He had the most charming dimple in his cheek when he smiled.

"The paranormal world is definitely complicated," Gunther agreed. "While I understand the complications and rivalries, I don't want it to be like that when I become ringmaster. I see my father's anger and resentment and secrecy and paranoia, and it just doesn't seem like a happy way to live."

"Yeah, I can understand that."

Gunther and I continued strolling through the open field as the sun continued its slow slide beneath the horizon. Suddenly, Gunther held his hand out gently to stop my walk. "Charlotte, I don't want you to see me as an enemy. I don't want to see you as an enemy."

"I don't, Gunther, really." Gunther was far too cute, blond, and charming to be my enemy, and he was also the first person I met since becoming ringmaster that didn't *depend* on me somehow. Uncle Phil depended on me to become the new ringmaster, and everyone else that I encountered within the Magical Midway needed that, too. Gunther didn't seem to want anything from me other than my friendship.

He is still Roland Makepeace's son, Samson interjected. *Do not become too comfortable with the young man.* I didn't respond.

"That's good. I hope you still feel that way after a few more interactions with my father." Gunther stuck his hands in his pockets and turned toward the clear late afternoon sky, squinting as he stared into the distance. "My father really wants to be the only ringmaster. I don't know why. Greed, maybe?"

"You don't have a very good relationship with your father, do you?"

"I love my father. He's my father. But no, we don't have a good relationship. We are...we are very different people."

"Whatever his reasons, it doesn't matter. I have too many people depending on me to allow this place to fall," I told him.

"The Witches' Council definitely wants to see

us both fall. At least a portion of the Council, anyway."

"Mina, Mabel, and Mercy already paid me a visit. I was not impressed." I made a face and Gunther laughed.

"Ah, yes, the terrible triplets. While they are somewhat amusing, they are also formidable enemies. I wanted to talk to you about your magical training primarily because of them."

"Oh?"

"Since you are the ringmaster, you can't leave here for more than a day or two, so you don't even have the option of going to any of the Witches Academies now. Even if you did, I don't think you would want to. It would give the terrible triplets too much information about your strengths and weaknesses. They would use that. Without a doubt."

"It seems a little late to talk about going to school, anyway. I mean, I'm almost thirty."

"And yet without that training, you are at a distinct disadvantage. You have to depend on the Midway to protect you—and as you can see with what happened to your uncle, that can't always be relied upon."

I shuddered. Just a few days ago, I felt

practically omnipotent. Well, people claimed I was almost omnipotent. As the days passed, nothing about being the ringmaster seemed to be as it was originally presented. My own talent echoed the truth of what Gunther was saying. If he wasn't right, he believed wholeheartedly that he was.

"Okay, so if you were me, what would you do?"

"I would let a ringmaster heir teach me the magic that I need to know," Gunther smiled and stepped back to bow formally. "You'd honestly be doing me a favor. In teaching you the magic I think you need to know, you'll be helping me to see the circus differently. My father runs the Makepeace Circus with an iron fist and a tyrant's attitude. That's not who I want to be."

"Wouldn't your father be angry at you? If he found out you were helping me, I mean."

"No doubt. That's why I plan to tell Dad I'm getting close to you to spy on you. Which is *kind of* the truth? Just not for the reasons he would assume." Gunther turned and held out his hands. "So, what you think?"

The young man is sincere in his offer, Samson said.

I know, I can sense it.

Can you also sense he finds you pretty? While his

offer is sincere, he harbors some additional agendas he is not entirely as forthcoming about, Samson said.

Oh? I asked as I blushed. *You can sense that?*

His familiar Delilah is quite the chatterbox. No need to sense anything when she's happy to let me know he's talked about you to her extensively.

"I think I'd like to know more about the circuses beyond just my family's view of it, too, I guess," I told Gunther after a pause. "I also don't like having to depend on anything I don't understand for my own self-defense. Maybe it's a good idea to have a backup, you know?"

"So, we're doing it?" Gunther asked with a smile.

"Yep, let's do it."

"Fantastic." We shook hands formally and laughed.

"I really do appreciate your willingness to teach me," I told him as we walked back toward the residential area. "The offer was really generous, especially since I've never been trained at all."

"I think I'll get quite a bit out of it, too," Gunther told me hopefully. "Dust off the old wand and practice my own skills. At the very least, I'll get to leave my father's Midway frequently."

"Is your circus all *that* different from ours?"

Gunther's face fell as he gazed down at the ground. Seconds passed, and I could feel his discomfort at my question. After two dozen steps, he sighed. "Yes. Yes, our circus is much different from yours."

"Well, maybe as part of my lessons, I can come to visit, and you can show me around."

Gunther nodded and fell silent again. His openness had given way to an almost palpable melancholy.

"Perhaps," he said quietly, and as we walked together, I sensed the first deliberate lie from my new friend.

After an optimistic family dinner, most of the participants drifted away. Eventually, only my family and my familiar remained around the dining table. A dining table that seemed like it shrank again, by the way. At the Magical Midway, everyday magic was something I would have to learn to get used to.

"So, Charlotte, are you still comfortable with your decision?" my mother asked as she dug into a chocolate sundae. "It seems like you had an incredibly exciting first few days. Any regrets?"

"I miss you guys," I told her as I squeezed her hand. "No regrets, though. I've been so isolated for so much of my life in a lot of ways. Even though I could sense what people were thinking, or at least the emotions behind them, my life was kind of empty except for you guys. It was hard to get close to people."

"You do seem to have made some friends here," my father observed. "You never really talked about anyone except Fiona when you came home from your visits."

"I didn't really get out much. Since I was only here a week, there never seemed to be much point."

"I'm glad to see that you're making friends," my mother said. "And, oh my, that Gunther is a handsome young man! I think he likes you, Charlotte."

"Martha, we don't want to encourage that," my father told her, shifting in his chair. "Gunther will eventually be the ringmaster of the Makepeace Circus."

"What does that have to do with anything?"

"Once he is the ringmaster, he can't leave his Midway for more than a day, the same as

Charlotte can't leave hers. What kind of relationship would that be for the two of them? A tragic one, that's what kind of relationship," my father told my mother.

As my parents discussed the pros and cons of my possible romantic relationship with Gunther, I rolled my eyes. The two of them could make a mountain out of a molehill even when there was no mole in sight.

Sure, Gunther was handsome. He seemed kind. Eventually, we would be the only two people on the planet with the responsibility to carry the magic of the Midway. We got along. We would be working together to teach me magic. But that didn't mean we would fall for each other.

What your father has said is true, Samson said. *If there is a kernel of care within you for Gunther, you would be well advised to snuff it out.*

I don't have time for a relationship, so this is all pointless.

Love has a way of popping up just when you decide you don't need it, Uncle Phil interjected as my parents continued arguing out loud whether it would be a good idea or a bad idea for me to date Roland Makepeace's son. *It's a good idea for you to know of the potential issues before you get too attached to the young man.*

"Could everyone just stop? Stop debating my love life, stop thinking things about my love life in my direction. Just stop. Let's just enjoy the rest of this evening without going over the pros and cons of a relationship that's not even happening. Okay?"

They murmured their agreement and changed the subject to what Uncle Phil could and could not do while dead.

As they clinked glasses and laughed at each other's jokes, I enjoyed the first meal I ever had with my family that included no argument between the Astley brothers over my future. It was unnervingly peaceful. I didn't even mind my parents' debate over my nonexistent future with Gunther so much.

Tomorrow, the sun would rise over the Magical Midway. There were things I needed to do that I wasn't even sure how to get done. In two days, the humans would again flood the Midway, and I would be challenged once more. The Witches' Council would visit again, and Roland Makepeace was an unknown. I had things to worry about, and the path forward as the new ringmaster I needed to find.

For tonight, though, life was good.

THANK YOU FOR READING!
I hope you enjoyed Witchiest Circus on Earth!
Please think about leaving a review. Ready for
more? Grab the next book in the series, Life on
the Lion.

KEEP UP WITH LEANNE LEEDS

Thanks so much for reading. I hope you liked it. Want to keep up with me? Text me at 1-512-359-3123 to get updates, info, or to shoot me a question.

You can also visit leanneleeds.com to:

Find all my books…

Sign up for my newsletter…

Like me on Facebook…

Follow me on Twitter…

Follow me on Instagram…

Thanks again for reading!

Leanne Leeds

FIND A TYPO? LET US KNOW!

Typos happen. It's sad, but true.

Though we go over the manuscript multiple times, have editors, have beta readers, and advance readers it's inevitable that determined typos and mistakes sometimes find their way into a published book.

Did you find one? If you did, think about reporting it on leanneleeds.com so we can get it corrected.